How Can I
Be a Detective
If I Have to
Babysit?

HOW CAN I BE A DETECTIVE IF I HAVE TO BABYSIT?

LINDA BAILEY

SCHOLASTIC INC.

New York Toronto London Auckland Sydney
Mexico City New Delhi Hong Kong

ISBN 0-590-30389-9

Text copyright © 1993 by Linda Bailey.
Cover illustration copyright © 1997 by Greg Thorkelson.
All rights reserved.
Published by Scholastic Inc., 555 Broadway, New York, NY 10012,
by arrangement with Albert Whitman & Company.
SCHOLASTIC and associated logos are trademarks and/or registered
trademarks of Scholastic Inc.

12 11 10 9 8 7 6 5 4 3 2 1   9/9 0 1 2 3 4/0

Printed in the U.S.A.   40

First Scholastic printing, May 1999

Thanks to my first-draft readers: Tess Grainger, Lia Grainger, Jessica Snodgrass, Shonali Chakrabarti, Derek Allan, Sara Sufrin.

Many thanks, too, to that finest and funniest of editors, Charis Wahl.

Kids Can Press Ltd. acknowledges with appreciation the assistance of the Canada Council and the Ontario Arts Council in the production of this book.

Edited by Charis Wahl at Kids Can Press.
Interior design by Tom Dart/First Folio Resource Group, Inc.

For Bill with love

CHAPTER

T HE MOMENT I MET ALEXANDER, I SMELLED trouble. Alexander Creely was *exactly* the kind of kid who could ruin a person's whole wilderness holiday.

How did I know? There were three obvious clues:

1. He was five years old.
2. He was holding a loaded squirt gun the size of my arm.
3. He seemed to think I'd come all the way to Ruby Lake just to play cops and robbers with *him*.

"C'mon, Stevie, let's try it! You be the robber, and I'll be the cop! You run and I'll chase you! C'mon — run! It'll be fun!" He raised his giant squirt gun and aimed it into my face.

"Alexander! If you squirt me with that thing, you'll be —"

SPLAT!

"Aw, Stevie . . . why didn't you run?"

I'm Stevie Diamond. Aged twelve. Female. Private detective — and I'm not talking about *playing* detective, either.

Me and my partner, Jesse Kulniki, had already solved an important crime and caught this crook who stole almost a thousand bucks. We'd been in the newspapers and everything. So it was downright insulting — *insulting!* — to be expected to play cops and robbers with a five-year-old. After I dried my head off, that's exactly what I told my dad.

"This was supposed to be a big adventure for me and Jesse, Dad. We want to take off alone. Go hiking and canoeing. Maybe do some fishing."

Jesse and I were visiting my dad in his tree-planting camp. It was way, way out there in the B.C. mountains — nothing but a bunch of tents and campers set up in an old forestry campsite. The tree planters lived there for the spring season. Every day they'd go off in trucks to plant trees on the mountain slopes. My dad was their supervisor, so he'd go, too. That meant that — except for the camp cooks — Jesse and I would be on our own. Free! We could do anything we wanted! Anything! Except for . . .

Alexander!

My dad shrugged. "He's got as much right to be here as you, Stevie. After all, his mom *is* head cook." He raised an eyebrow. "Don't you think it would be a good idea to stay on her good side?"

I could see his point. I didn't want to starve to death while I was here.

"Anyway, what's the problem?" he went on.

"You're all kids. Why can't you and Jesse and Alexander have a good time together?"

"Dad! He's five! He's young enough for me to baby-sit!"

"Okay, fine. You and Jesse can be Alexander's baby-sitters while you're here."

I groaned. "I *hate* baby-sitting! When they had a baby-sitting course at school, everyone in my whole class signed up except me. I'd rather deliver papers, I'd rather mow lawns, I'd rather feed hunks of raw meat to starving tigers, I'd —"

"Okay, I get the point. You don't like baby-sitting."

"I do," said Jesse, strolling up behind my dad. "I enjoy hanging around with little kids."

"Thanks a lot, Jesse Kulniki," I muttered.

"Oh, come on. Alexander's not so bad. And we've got all this!" Jesse waved at the lake, silver blue and sparkling in the sunlight, and at the huge Douglas firs towering on the other side. "How could we possibly have a rotten time? Even with Alexander?"

"Jesse's right," said my dad. "Think about it, Stevie. You two could be in school right now. It's still a month away from summer holidays."

"Yeah," said Jesse, "if we were in school today, we'd be learning about the — uh, let's see — the major exports of Saskatchewan."

I have to admit, the idea of missing the major exports of Saskatchewan *did* cheer me up.

Besides being partners in crime, Jesse and I are in the same grade and live in the same housing co-op in Vancouver. When my dad invited us to visit him in tree-planting camp, we got really excited. Jesse, especially. He lives with his mom, and she doesn't like the outdoors much, so he'd hardly even been camping before. All the way through the nine-hour bus trip to Revelstoke (which we took all on our own), the smile never left his face. He kept talking about the wilderness as if it had a capital *W*. Like he'd say, "You've got to be prepared when you go into the Wilderness" or "It's no piece of cake, you know, going off into the Wilderness."

This Wilderness stuff was kind of dumb, but I'd smiled, too. All the way to Revelstoke. All through the truck ride north after my dad picked us from the bus. All the way to Spruce River and then north again another thirty-five kilometres to Ruby Lake. All the way up till the moment I met . . . Alexander!

"Look at it this way," said my dad. "Alexander's here to stay. You can have a good time with him or a lousy time. It's up to you."

I thought about this. Maybe baby-sitting wouldn't be so bad. True, I'd never taken the course at school, but I *had* read a couple of books about girls who baby-sat a lot. Maybe I could remember a trick or two from those books. After all, how hard could baby-sitting a five-year-old possibly be?

"Okay," I said slowly. "I'll *try* to be nice to him."

"That's great." My dad smiled with relief. "Now if you two get your stuff unpacked, you might have time for a swim before dinner."

Jesse and I headed down the path to our camper. As I pushed through the overgrown branches, I could hear him clanking behind me. "Honestly, Jesse! Do you really think you're going to *need* all that stuff?"

Before we left Vancouver, Jesse had put together what he called his "Wilderness outfit." He was wearing a checked shirt, old army pants and a pair of knee-high rubber boots — even though it hadn't rained for weeks. The pants had all these belt loops, and Jesse had hung a bunch of "emergency supplies" from them: a compass, a Swiss Army knife, a water bottle, a whistle, a snake-bite kit and a package of wooden matches sealed in a plastic bag. On his head was this squashed-looking yellow hat covered in swimming badges that he kept calling his "lucky fishing hat." A huge pair of binoculars dangled from his neck, which — being on the skinny side — couldn't exactly handle the load. His head tilted forward like a turtle's.

"This is all important stuff," he said. "You never know what you're going to run into way out here —"

"In the Wilderness. Yeah, yeah, I know."

"You should wear a hat," he went on. "Anybody with as many freckles as you is going to get *toasted* the first time the sun —"

"No way. I tan — golden brown!" What was he talking about, anyway? I have exactly twenty-one freckles on my whole face. Twenty, if you don't count the one under my nose, which is actually — if you look close — a beauty spot.

"Yowtch!" I stopped short as my hair grabbed on to a branch.

"Don't move. I *told* you you should wear a hat."

So then I had to stand there while Jesse carefully pulled my hair loose, strand by strand. My hair is really thick and curly and bushy. Even in the city, it does pretty much whatever it wants. Out in the woods, it goes wild — grabbing branches, catching seeds, gobbling twigs. They could make a movie about it — *The Hair That Ate British Columbia.*

I mumbled a thank-you to Jesse as I pulled free of the branch. A minute later, we stepped into the clearing. My dad always likes to set up camp away from other people, and right now I was glad. At least Jesse and I could get away on our own. Right?

Wrong.

Out of the camper doorway popped a small blond head. "Boo!" said Alexander. "Where were you? I been waiting and waiting and *waiting* for you guys." He stared at us accusingly over the tops of his glasses. They drooped halfway down his nose and were covered in smears.

"What are *you* doing in our camper?"

"Psst!" Jesse nudged me in the ribs. "You told your dad you were going to be nice."

I sighed and tried to remember the girls in the baby-sitting books. What would they do? Cops and robbers, that was it. Stretching my lips into what I hoped was a friendly smile, I began again. "Excuse me, uh, Captain of the Cops. The Captain of the, uh, Robbers would like to get into the — the police station."

It worked. Too well. A huge grin swept across Alexander's face. As I stepped into the camper, he threw both his arms around my waist and squeezed. For a little kid, he was awfully strong. It felt as if a boa constrictor had fallen in love with me.

"You're nice, Stevie," he said into my stomach. "But we're not playing cops and robbers any more."

He pulled his face out of my T-shirt. His glasses looked a tiny bit cleaner. My T-shirt looked a tiny bit dirtier. "We're playing spy club now," he said. "You can be in the club, but only if you do the special spy-club chant."

"Gee, thanks a bunch." I peeled him off and went into the camper. "Maybe later."

"Want to watch us unpack?" Jesse asked.

"Oh goody," said Alexander. "I love seeing other people's stuff. Say, isn't this a neat camper? It's got this little weeny sink, like a toy sink, but it runs real water. See this? And here's Stevie's daddy's stove. And here's Stevie's daddy's fridge. And in this cupboard is —"

"I know," I interrupted. "Stevie's daddy's dishes. This is *my* camper, remember?"

Alexander just kept chattering. "And here's where Stevie's daddy keeps the forks, and here's where Stevie's daddy keeps the pots, and here's —"

Jesse pulled his suitcase open. Taking out a neatly folded pair of pyjamas, he hung them in the closet my dad had reserved for him.

I stared into his suitcase. "Did your mom pack your stuff?"

"No, I did it myself. Why?"

"You're kidding! It's all folded!"

"Of course," he said, looking surprised.

I shook my head, grabbed my knapsack and headed for the back of the camper. My bed was up in a kind of loft with a curtain you can pull shut. Usually, my mom and dad slept up there. But now, since I was the only girl in the camper, I'd get the loft bed to myself. Jesse and my dad would get the bunk beds in the front.

Behind me, I could hear Alexander chattering. "Whatzat, Jesse? A T-shirt? Where'd you get it? How many T-shirts you got, Jesse? I got about a zillion. Whatzat? Socks? I got lotsa socks. Blue ones, red ones, all kinds. Whatzat? Wow, a toothbrush. I got a Peter Rabbit toothbrush. I used to have a Winnie-the-Pooh toothbrush, but I used it on my dog, and then I had to get a new one. Hey, whatzat, Jesse?"

Closing my ears, I hauled my pack up to the loft and unzipped it. Then I dumped everything out — clothes, books, games. It made a huge pile in the middle of my bed. I lay down with my head on my pillow and put my feet against the pile, bending my legs at the knee. Letting out a grunt, I pushed as hard as I could with my feet. It only took three quick shoves to get all the stuff down to the bottom of the bed.

"There!" I said. "Unpacked!"

Jesse just shook his head. But Alexander was up in my loft in a flash. "Lemme see *your* stuff, Stevie. What'd you bring? Anything good? Whatzat?"

"Nothing you'd be interested in, Alexander." I took a deep breath and remembered my responsibilities as a baby-sitter. Wasn't there something in those books about keeping parents informed? "Does your mom know you're here? Maybe she's looking for you."

"She told me to come back at five. Is it five yet?" Alexander's foot shot out into the air and stopped about two centimetres from my face.

I jerked my head backwards. "I have no idea, Alexander. Would you mind getting your foot out of my nose?"

"But that's where my watch is."

"What? Up my nose?"

"No, Stevie — har, har. You're funny. Har, har, har." Alexander was so struck by the idea that he did a half somersault, shrieking and gurgling with laughter. "It's on my ankle," he said finally, when he'd caught his breath. "See?" He hauled up his pant leg. Strapped around his ankle was a Ralph the Robot Rat wristwatch.

Ralph the Robot Rat is this cartoon character that a lot of kids — mostly boys — are really into these days. He has this long, pointy metal nose and spiky metal ears, and he's always rescuing other animals from the Killer Cats. Killer Cats are these huge, fat metal guys with rows of needle-sharp teeth. They pick on little wimpy animals — mice, for instance, and gerbils and squirrels. The Killer Cats are way bigger than Ralph the Robot Rat, but it doesn't make any difference. Good old Ralph always knocks them flat in the end. Lots of boys I know have Ralph the Robot Rat stuff — watches, T-shirts, pencil cases. You can even get Ralph the Robot Rat cereal.

"This may be a dumb question," I said to Alexander, "but why are you wearing a wristwatch around your ankle?"

"'Cause it fits!" yelled Alexander. "I used to have it around my wrist, but it fell off all the time." He showed me his wrist. It was bigger than a pencil, but not much.

"Hey!" Jesse had just spotted the watch. He grinned. "Snick, snick, booga, booga, snick, snick!"

"Beg your pardon?" I said.

"Snick, snick, booga, booga, snick, snick." Alexander practically squealed it back at him.

"What are you guys talking about?"

The two of them did something weird with their fingers and noses. "Snick, snick," said Jesse in a low whispering voice.

"Booga, booga," said Alexander in the same kind of voice.

"What the heck is going on here?" I demanded.

Jesse glanced up as if he'd forgotten I was there. "It's what Ralph the Robot Rat says just before he fights a Killer Cat. Snick, snick, booga, booga, snick, snick."

"Snick, snick? He actually says snick, snick?"

"It's the secret chant for the spy club," said Alexander.

Now I was totally confused. "*What* spy club?"

"The Ralph the Robot Rat Spy Club!" he yelled.

Jesse looked a teeny bit embarrassed. "It's all over the world," he explained. "When you meet other members, you say the chant and you recognize each other."

"We can make you a member, too, Stevie." Alexander was leaping around on my bed. "You just have to say the secret chant three times."

"Thanks, Alexander," I said, shaking my head. "I think I'll pass."

He stopped jumping. His mouth drooped. His eyes drooped. Even his cheeks drooped. "Does that mean no?"

Jesse gave me a look — I was being a Bad Baby-sitter. "Come on, Stevie. All you have to do is say the chant. It's no big deal."

"That's it? Just the chant? Nothing else?"

"I swear," said Jesse, putting his hand over his heart. "Nothing else."

"Except for the salute," said Alexander.

"Salute?" I said. "What salute?"

They both raised their pointer fingers on each hand and put them in front of their noses, making them stick out straight ahead.

"What's *that* supposed to be?" I said.

"Rats' noses," said Jesse. "Just do it, okay, Stevie?"

I sighed and stuck two fingers out in front of my nose. "Snick, snick," I mumbled under my breath. "Booga, booga. Snick, snick. Okay?"

"Two more times," said Alexander. "Louder!"

"Snick, snick, booga, booga, snick, snick. Snick, snick, booga, booga, snick, snick." I couldn't believe I was actually doing this.

"Hooray!" yelled Alexander. "You're a member of the Ralph the Robot Rat Spy Club, Stevie." He jumped up and down.

"Take it easy, Alexander. You're going to break my bed."

Jesse was lining up books on a shelf, and I climbed down to check them out. *Birds of*

Western Canada. Grant's Bird Guide. Butterflies and Moths.

"Is this all you've got?" I knew Jesse was a bird lover, but I didn't know he was interested in butterflies, too. "Didn't you bring any mysteries?"

"I couldn't fit everything in," he said. "And I knew you'd bring mysteries."

He was right. *The Marmalade Murders. Ghosts in the Garage. The Case of the One-Legged Tap Dancer.* If things got really dull with Alexander, I could always curl up with a good book.

Jesse was laughing at something in my loft. I glanced around.

Alexander! Wearing *my* brand-new bathing suit. Stretched over the top of his head, like a helmet, were *my* brand-new rainbow-patterned underpants. "Look at me! I'm a space man," he yelled.

"Alexander!" I was up in the loft like a shot, snatching my underwear off his head and yanking the bathing suit off him in two quick jerks. "Out!" I yelled. "Right now!"

"But, Stevie, I haven't seen all your stuff yet. I haven't even —"

"Out! And you, Jesse Kulniki, you stop laughing!"

"Who's laughing?" he asked as he helped Alexander down from the loft. Okay, he wasn't laughing. But his face had that expression a face gets when it's trying really hard not to laugh — with the cheeks all sucked in. "Alexander's just playing dress-up, Stevie. All little kids play dress-up."

"Fine!" I said. "He can play dress-up in *your* underwear."

"I wanna go for a swim." Alexander hopped onto the bottom bunk — my dad's — and bounced up and down on it. A pillow flew onto the floor. "Can we go swimming in the lake?"

"Great idea," said Jesse, hauling Alexander off the bunk. "But you can't wear Stevie's bathing suit, understand? She needs it. Hey, Stevie, want to go for a swim?"

I was steaming. Ready to boil over. Maybe a jump in the lake would cool me down. I yanked the curtains of the loft shut. After taking a peek to make sure Alexander was at the far end of the camper, I quickly slipped out of my clothes. I was sitting there naked, one foot stuck in my bathing suit, when I noticed the eye.

Alexander's. It was peeking through the gap in the curtain.

Then I saw the hand. Alexander's. It grabbed a handful of curtain material.

Before I could move or say a word, the curtain flew open. Wide open! For just a second, I could see Jesse's face. Staring. Eyes huge. Mouth open. Then he whirled around, and all I could see was his back.

"It's okay, Stevie. I didn't see a thing! Honest, I didn't!"

Too shocked to move, I just sat there, one foot still stuck in my bathing suit. Alexander — can you *believe* this? — started tugging on my big toe. "Hey, Stevie! Hurry up! Finish changing so we can go swimming. Stevie? What's wrong?"

I didn't even open my mouth. I was afraid of what might come out. Slowly, I unfastened

Alexander's fingers from my toe. Carefully, I pulled the curtains shut. I yanked on my clothes and jumped down from the loft. Grabbing Alexander by the hand, I headed for the door. Jesse followed — probably to make sure I didn't strangle Alexander.

"Where're we going, Stevie?" asked Alexander. "Aren't we going swimming? Where's your bathing suit?"

I didn't say a word. Not until we were standing in front of my dad — me, Jesse and Alexander.

"That's it," I said. "I've had it!"

My dad was sitting at a table in the cook tent, sorting through papers. The place was filled with delicious dinner smells, but I was so mad I hardly even noticed. Standing at a counter was Alexander's mom, Milly. She looked like a grown-up version of Alexander, with a round face, a short little nose and big blue eyes behind a huge pair of glasses. Her long blond hair was pulled back in a pony-tail. She was wearing a yellow apron, and her hands were in a big bowl full of water and lettuce.

I didn't care if she was his mom. I didn't care if she was the head cook. I was so mad, I wouldn't have cared if she was the Queen of England! I blurted out everything — the squirt gun, the foot in my face, my underwear, my bathing suit. When I got to the part about the curtain flying open, my dad's face got that same expression that Jesse's had had, cheeks all sucked in.

"Dad! It's not funny! It's horrible."

My dad's face straightened out. "Sorry, Stevie."

He turned to Alexander. "When Stevie closes the curtain on the loft, Alexander, that means she wants privacy."

"Sorry," said Alexander in a voice you could hardly hear.

Milly put her arms around him. "Oh, now, Stevie, Alexander's only five. He didn't mean anything. He was just playing, weren't you, Alexander?"

"Yeah." Alexander's glasses drooped down his nose again, and he shoved them back up. "I was playing spy. I was spying on Stevie."

I couldn't believe it. "See what I mean, Dad? Ever since we got here, he's been after me to play these dumb kid games. Cops and robbers! Spy! Ralph the Robot Rat! I'm twelve years old, for crying out loud. Jesse and I are *real* detectives! I'm tired of playing dorky little games with a dorky little kid!"

Alexander charged up to me and stuck his face as close as he could get it to mine. "Oh yeah?" he yelled. "Real detectives, huh? I bet you couldn't catch a *real* criminal. You could never in a million years catch Mr. Patchouli! He's a —"

"Alexander!" said Milly. "Stop it!"

"What?" I stammered. Criminal? Mr. Patchouli?

"Mr. Patchouli is a smuggler!" yelled Alexander. "And he lived in *our* house! The police are after him. That's how come we came here. Tell them, Mommy!"

Milly didn't say a word.

"Mommy?" said Alexander, his voice suddenly tiny and uncertain. "Mommy?"

CHAPTER

2

"O H DEAR," SAID MILLY FINALLY.

"Milly?" My dad looked worried. "Are you all right?"

Milly wagged a finger at her son. "Alexander, you know I didn't want to talk about this!"

Alexander hung his head. The glasses slid to the end of his nose. "I forgot."

"Mr. Patchouli!" Milly let out an enormous sigh. "Every time I hear that name, I break out in hives. Look!" She held out an arm. I couldn't see anything except a piece of green onion stuck to her elbow.

Turning to my dad, she said, "If you ever get a notion to rent your house out to a stranger, Mike — don't do it!"

My dad looked as confused as I felt. "What happened, Milly?"

She began twisting her apron ties between her fingers. "It all began in February when my mother got sick. She lives in Edmonton, you see, and she needed a gallstone operation. My father isn't well, either — with his high blood pressure and all — and I wanted to help out, so I decided to take Alex and move to Edmonton for a couple of months."

"That was, uh, very good of you," my dad said. He still sounded confused. So was I. I wished she'd get to the point.

"A friend of mine suggested I could save money by renting out the house while we were gone. So I put an ad in the newspaper."

"And this . . . this Mr. Patchouli showed up?" my dad suggested helpfully.

"Oh, no! He phoned! Long distance — from Hong Kong. Said he'd picked up a copy of the *Vancouver Sun* there. Isn't that amazing? You can buy a Vancouver newspaper halfway around the world! Anyway, he said his name was Peter Patchouli, and he needed a house in Vancouver for exactly the time we were going to be away. I described the house to him — I was very honest, mind you, and told him all about the leaky shower and the dishwasher that doesn't work. He said not to worry, it would be perfect. He sounded so polite. How was I to *know?*"

Milly was staring directly at me. She seemed to be waiting for an answer. I shrugged in what I hoped was an encouraging fashion. Encouraging her to get to the *point!*

"So you rented your house to this Mr. Patchouli over the phone?" my dad said.

Milly nodded. "He sent me a cheque for the full two months' rent. I cashed it, and Alexander and I flew to Edmonton the next day."

"But what about the key?" I asked. "How did he get into your house?"

"He said on the phone that he wouldn't arrive in time to pick up the key from me. He asked me to leave it in a post-office box at the main Vancouver post office."

"So you never saw him at all?" said Jesse.

Milly shook her head. "How was I to *know?* He sounded so nice. He even offered to water our plants."

"Of course you couldn't know," said my dad, although it sounded pretty dumb to me — going off and leaving the key to your house for someone you'd never even met!

Milly pulled a tissue out of her apron pocket and blew her nose. "Alex and I flew to Edmonton, and my mother had her gallstone surgery. It takes a lot out of you, you know, to have surgery at her age, but the doctor said she'd be back on her feet in no time, especially if she took care and got plenty of rest and —"

I couldn't stand it any longer. "What about Mr. Patchouli?" I guess my voice came out pretty loud.

"Oh!" said Milly with a start. "Oh yes, Mr. Patchouli! Well, we hadn't been in Edmonton two weeks, when what do you think happened? The police showed up. At my parents' house! In Edmonton! I was mortified."

"What did they want?" asked Jesse.

"They wanted to question me!" Milly looked shocked. "They seemed to think I was part of some sort of, of, smuggling ring! Me — sneaking things into the country illegally! Can you imagine?"

No, I couldn't. Milly was the type who, if her kid snuck a grape in the supermarket, she'd insist on paying for it.

"It's that Mr. Patchouli," said Milly. "He's wanted by the police in seven different countries! He's an international smuggler. And his name isn't even Patchouli! It's Ragnall — Ronald Ragnall!"

"Gosh," said Jesse. His eyes were huge. "Did the police arrest him? Did they track him down to your house in Vancouver?"

Milly nodded. "My neighbours told me that three police cars came. Three! A whole crowd of police rushed the front and back doors at the same time. Tramped right through my tulip and daffodil beds!"

"What happened?" I asked.

"He was gone!" Milly cried. "There was no one there. But he must have run off in a big hurry. He left his suitcase and clothes behind. And a half-eaten pizza — still warm on the table."

"What kind of pizza?" asked Jesse. I groaned. He was as bad as Milly. Who *cared* what kind of pizza?

"I have no idea," said Milly. "All I know is, when we got home the next day, it was smelling up the whole kitchen. I threw it out. Uggh!"

"It was olive," whispered Alexander. "And that yucky fishy stuff. Anch — what do you call it?"

"Anchovy," Jesse whispered back.

My dad sighed. "Well, anyway, it must have felt good to come home and get your life back to normal." My dad's not great at listening to long stories. I could tell he was trying really hard to be understanding.

"But it *isn't* back to normal!" said Milly. "That's just the point! For days after we got back, the police were all over the house — moving furniture around, hauling pictures off the walls, dumping fingerprint powder everywhere. They turned the couch upside-down, they pulled books out of the bookcase — they even took my toaster apart! The whole place was a shambles."

"Wow!" said Jesse. "Why'd they do all that?"

"Can't you see?" I said. It was so obvious. "Mr. Patchouli — I mean Ragnall — is a smuggler. He left in a hurry. He must have left something valuable behind — or, at least, the police thought so."

"What did he leave?" asked Jesse.

"I haven't the slightest idea!" Milly's face was cherry pink and puffy. Maybe she really *would* break out in hives. "They wouldn't tell me. They didn't seem to believe me when I told them how I rented the house."

Not surprising, I thought — a mysterious phone call from Hong Kong, a cheque in the mail, a key in a post-office box. The police probably thought it was a pretty fishy story.

"But I did find out a few things from the newspaper." Milly disappeared into the kitchen area and returned with her purse.

"Here!" She pulled a crumpled piece of newspaper out of her wallet and threw it on the table. "I cut this out the day after we got back. Just look what a — a horrible crook we had living in our house!"

The headline of the newspaper article said RUBBERFACE RAGNALL AT LARGE. I picked it up and began reading aloud. "'Vancouver police are searching for Ronald Ragnall, an internationally wanted smuggler currently believed to be in the Vancouver area. Ragnall was holed up until today at 1313 Lilac Street, where police attempted unsuccessfully to make an arrest.'"

"You see?" Milly interrupted. "Our address! Holed up! In *our* house!"

Clearing my throat, I continued. "'Ragnall, a master of disguise, is known in police circles as "Rubberface" Ragnall. He is said to have the ability to transform his appearance almost completely. He goes by a number of aliases —'"

"Whatzat?" Alexander cut in.

"Fake names," I snapped in what was definitely a Bad Baby-sitter voice. I continued reading. "'He goes by a number of aliases, including Peter Patchouli, Bobby Zamboni and Nestor Mazurka. According to police, Ragnall has smuggled millions of dollars' worth of illegal items into North America over the past five years, mostly from Asian countries.'"

"Gosh!" Jesse interrupted. "I wonder what he smuggles."

"If you'd just *listen*," I said, "you might find out."

"Sorry."

I continued reading. "'Police say that the smuggled items include gold, silver, precious gems, exotic birds, computer software and objects of fine art. Vancouver police are currently questioning the owner of the house where Ragnall has been hiding — a Ms. Millicent Creely.'"

"You see?" Milly's voice was shrill. "My name! In the newspaper! Like a common criminal!"

"Oh, now, Milly," said my dad. "Surely things calmed down after the police completed their search."

"Calmed down?" said Milly. "Calmed down? That was only the *beginning!*"

"He came back," said Alexander in a hushed voice. "Mr. Patchouli came back!"

"What?" I said. "With police all over the place?"

"He waited," said Milly, "till the police were gone. Alex and I went out shopping one afternoon. When we came home — what do you think? Our whole house was turned upside-down again. Books and furniture thrown around, everything a mess. I thought the police had come back. But when I called, they didn't know a thing about it. It was that awful man — Mr. Patchouli, or Mr. Rubberface, or whatever his name is."

"I saw him!" Alexander blurted out. "When we came back from shopping! I ran into the kitchen, like this —" He raced halfway across the cook tent to show us, then charged back. "He was running away, across the backyard. He was wearing a dirty red raincoat. It had a hood." He stopped, and his eyes seemed to fill most of his face. "I saw him!" he repeated in a breathless voice.

Milly raised her eyebrows and snorted. "Now, Alexander, we're not *sure* you saw him. *I* looked in the backyard, and I didn't see a thing."

"I saw him!" insisted Alexander. "I did!"

"Of course you did, dear." She patted his head absent-mindedly. "It was that very night I broke out in hives. I began having nightmares, too. And poor Alexander, with his imagination — why, he was just scared to bits, weren't you, sweetie?"

Alexander grinned and nodded. He didn't look all that scared to me.

"But why did he come back?" Jesse asked. "Rubberface Ragnall? I mean, he'd already gotten away —"

"Don't you see?" I said. "He must have been looking for the same thing the police were looking for. Something he left behind!"

Milly shivered. "I just had to get away," she said. "The very next day I called my friend, Rhonda, at Totem Tree Planting, and she told me there was a cook's job available up here. I couldn't *wait* to get out of Vancouver! If the police — or this Rubberface fellow — want to ransack my house, at least I won't be around to see it."

She glanced down at her watch. "Oh, my goodness!" she said, jumping up. "Look at the time. The tree planters will be back any minute. They'll be starving."

My dad stood up, too. "Listen, Milly, I'm awfully sorry about all these problems. Is there any way I can help?"

"The only way you can help," said Milly, "is to forget the whole thing. I wouldn't have breathed a word if Alexander hadn't spoken up, and I don't want to talk about it any more. What we need now is peace and quiet."

"I understand," said my dad quietly. He picked up his papers. "We won't mention it again. Right, Stevie? Jesse?"

"Sure," said Jesse.

"Stevie?" Then again, a moment later, "Stevie?"

"What? Oh yeah. Right, Dad, sure."

But it was too late. My mind was already in full-speed detective mode. Questions and clues and ideas were hopping around in my brain like popcorn on a hot stove.

I just couldn't *wait* to get Alexander alone and quiz him!

CHAPTER

3

A VOICE FROM THE DOORWAY INTERRUPTED MY
thoughts. "Hi, guys!" A woman with long
curly hair the colour of tomato soup was
tying on a big green apron.

"Hi, Rebecca!" yelled Alexander. "Where you
been?"

"In my tent, kiddo, catching up on my sleep."
She glanced at Milly as she walked towards us.
"Sorry I'm late, Milly. I just can't get used to
waking up at four-thirty in the morning."

"Hmmph!" said Milly, without looking at her.
"Finish up the salads now and get started on the
garlic bread. If we're going to be ready on time,
you'll have to hop to it." She turned to Alexander.
"Goodness! Just look at your hands! Dirty right up
to the elbows. You come with me, young man."

Milly and Alexander left the cook tent, with my
dad close behind.

The red-haired woman shook her head as she
watched them go. "Gosh," she said softly, "no
matter what I do, I always seem to blow it."
Turning to me and Jesse, she tried to smile. She

31

was tiny — smaller than me — and had a thin little face with big grey eyes.

"I'm Rebecca," she said. "You must be Jesse." He nodded. "And you're Stevie, right? The one who reads mysteries?"

"How did you know?"

"Your dad told me. He saw me reading a mystery one day and —"

"You read mysteries, too?"

"Sure, all the time. Actually" — she looked embarrassed — "I always kind of wanted to be a detective myself." She laughed — a tinkly little laugh. "Well, not really a detective, I guess. A policewoman. I wanted to join the police force."

"How come you didn't?" asked Jesse.

She thought a moment before answering. "Just lazy, I guess. I ended up reading about detectives instead. I drive my boyfriend crazy — always with my nose in a book. What kind do *you* read, Stevie?"

"Any kind that's not too creepy or spooky. I like the ones by Agatha Christie, the ones with —"

"Hercule Poirot?" Rebecca grinned and clapped her hands. "He's my all-time favourite. I bet I've read every Hercule Poirot mystery ever written."

"Who's this . . . how do you say it? . . . this Hair-kyul Pwa-row guy?" asked Jesse.

"He's a famous detective," said Rebecca. "He's kind of short and —"

"Pudgy," I said, "and he has this huge moustache and a head shaped like —"

"An egg!" We both said it at the same time.

Rebecca laughed. "It's going to be fun having you guys around. But, listen, I'd better get to work now. What did Milly say? Hop to it?" She grinned and did a couple of little hops towards the kitchen.

"Hey!" said Jesse. "Cool shoes!"

I glanced down. Rebecca was wearing a pair of fantastic tiger-striped sneakers. They had thick black soles and orange-and-black leather tops. She held up a foot to show them off.

"I got them in a little shop in Vancouver called Jungle Duds. I have another pair with leopard spots, and I bought my boyfriend a pair with zebra stripes."

"Cool," I said, gazing at her feet in admiration. "But I bet they cost a fortune."

"You could save up for them. Save your . . . I don't know, your baby-sitting money or whatever."

"Uh-oh," said Jesse, catching the look on my face, "you used the *B* word."

"*B* word?"

"Baby-sitting. Stevie hates it. And her dad says we're supposed to baby-sit Alexander."

Rebecca started saying something about how she always had to baby-sit her little brother, and what a pain it was, but I wasn't paying attention. A thought had just hit me.

Baby-sitting! Why hadn't I figured it out before? It was perfect. What better way to get Alexander alone and question him about Rubberface Ragnall!

Rebecca had disappeared to the cooking corner of the tent — two fridges, two stoves and two sinks plus a lot of counters and shelves. She put a tape into a tape deck and started pulling things out of a fridge. Country music filled the tent.

I looked around. We were alone. Jesse and I could speak — detective to detective — without being overheard.

"Pssst!" I said in a low voice. "Are you thinking what I'm thinking?"

"What do you mean?"

"Rubberface Ragnall! A crime! A mystery!"

"But, Stevie, we promised your dad —"

"Oh, Jesse!" I stamped my foot. "How long have we been waiting for a chance like this?"

For six months, that's how long. Ever since we solved our first mystery, Jesse and I had been on the lookout for criminal activity. I guess I expected that after our first brilliant success, the mysteries would just drop into our laps — the way they do in books and movies. Take Nancy Drew, for instance. According to my calculations, she must have solved forty-eight crimes in her sixteenth year alone!

No such luck for me and Jesse. We'd hung around the bank for hours, hoping for a heist. We'd watched for suspicious-looking characters in our neighbourhood and followed a few of them till our feet were sore. We'd even stuck our business cards through every single mail slot in our co-op.

The closest we'd come to a crime was the time Phoebe Little got her favourite pink-and-white towel stolen from the co-op laundry room. After investigating for two whole days, we discovered that the towel wasn't even stolen. It just got tangled up with Hermione Krowser's pink-and-white sheets. Phoebe was very grateful when we brought the towel back — she even gave each of us a quarter. But, as Jesse said, it wasn't exactly what we had in mind when we formed the Diamond & Kulniki Detective Agency.

But smuggling — this was something real! Something serious! Something criminal!

"We'll call it . . . the Rubberface Ragnall case," I said softly.

"Case?" said Jesse. "What case? All this stuff happened miles away — in Vancouver! And probably weeks ago!"

"True," I said slowly. "But there's no reason why we can't quiz Alexander about his house and the phone call from Hong Kong and everything. Maybe we can figure out something the police missed!"

"Oh right!" said Jesse. "Two twelve-year-old detectives are going to solve a crime that the whole Vancouver police department can't solve. And we're going to do it from the other side of the province! From out in the middle of the Wilderness!"

The way he put it, it did sound a little discouraging. "Detectives don't always have to be right at the scene of the crime," I told him. "Look at Hercule Poirot. He solves crimes just by sitting in his office and using his little grey cells."

"Grey cells? Like in a prison? Dungeons?"

"Not that kind of cells!" I said. "The little grey cells in his *brain!* Hercule Poirot can figure out a mystery from miles away."

"Well, maybe *he* can," said Jesse. "But you're not Hercule Poirot! And neither am I. We're just a couple of —"

BLAAAAT! A truck horn sounded outside the tent. It was followed by a roar of engines.

"The tree planters!" I jumped up. "Listen, Jesse, we can talk more about the case later — when we're baby-sitting."

"Baby-sitting? You hate baby-sitting. And *what* case? We don't *have* a case." He was still muttering as he followed me outside.

A huge, mud-covered truck had just pulled into camp, and three more were close behind. Jesse and I watched the tree planters jump out — dozens of them. Their clothes, arms, hands and faces were covered in grey dirt and black soot, and their hair stood up all wild and shaggy. Some headed right for the showers — plastic cubicles hitched up to hoses that brought water from the lake. Others collapsed onto a wooden bench outside the cook tent.

"Wow!" said Jesse. "What *happened* to them?"

"Nothing," I said. "They've been working, that's all. You'll see tomorrow when we go out to watch."

Another truck pulled in, and more planters jumped out. Some of them I knew really well — the ones who had been planting with my dad for years. I got a few hugs — and dirt smears, too, but I didn't care. No one stays clean long in camp.

Soon the smells from the cook tent pulled Jesse and me back inside. Rebecca had laid out the food on a big table — a huge pot of bean soup, four enormous pans filled with two kinds of lasagna (meat and vegetarian), tossed salad, cole slaw, buttered green beans and tons of toasty hot garlic bread. The dessert was waiting behind the main course — a gigantic chocolate layer cake and apple cobbler with a big bowl of whipped cream.

"Fantastic!" said Jesse, helping himself to the vegetarian lasagna. "Is today special or is the food always this good?"

"Every day," I said. "Food's one of the most important things in a tree-planting camp. My dad says the planters have to have something to look forward to after working so hard all day."

Jesse took a second scoop of lasagna. "I figured I might have a problem, coming out here and being, you know, a vegetarian, but —"

His mouth dropped open as a group of planters came into the tent. The first three were all cleaned up and changed and looked like university students on vacation, which is what a lot of tree planters are. But the fourth planter!

If you wanted to explain what the word *creepy* meant, all you'd have to do is show a picture of this guy. He was tall and thin and bony and had this long straggly beard. His hair was ratty and tangled, too, and hung down past his neck. It was greyish brown like his beard. He was dressed in clothes so old and grimy you couldn't tell what they were made of. His nose was long and skinny and bent in the middle — as if it had been broken — and his tiny dark eyes gleamed in his face like coals.

"What's that on his cheek?" Jesse asked in a hushed voice.

I looked — without really looking, if you know what I mean. A scar ran down the right side of his face and disappeared into his collar.

"Who *is* he?" Jesse asked.

"Search me," I whispered back. "I've never seen him before."

When someone slapped me on the back, I jumped. It was Max, one of the planters I'd met last year. "Hey, there! Stephanie! Good to see you, kid!" Max was wearing jeans and a red sweatshirt. His thick brown hair was damp looking from his shower, and his freckled face was shiny. "You guys leave me any food?"

I introduced him to Jesse and, as soon as I got the chance, whispered, "Hey, Max, who's that? The guy with the beard and the scar?"

"Oh, you mean Mountain Man? Yeah, he's quite a sight. He's one of the new planters."

"New?" said Jesse. "He looks pretty old to me."

Max laughed. "Maybe forty or so — pretty old for a tree planter. But he's new to this crew. Stevie's dad hired him just a few days ago. You kids care to join me for dinner?"

Picking up our plates, we followed Max to one of the four long tables that took up most of the cook tent. "How come he just got hired?" Jesse asked.

"We picked up some extra work," Max said, as he gulped down his soup. "Stevie's dad hired four new planters in Revelstoke. Greeners."

"What's a greener?" asked Jesse.

"Someone who's new," I told him. "They're 'green' because they don't really know how to plant yet."

I watched Mountain Man heap his plate high and grab a glass of water. He sat in the far corner, all by himself. Strange.

"So tell me about this Mountain Man," I said to Max. "Who is he? Where'd he come from?"

"Lives off by himself in the woods," said Max, munching on a mouthful of salad. "Somewhere in the Kootenay Mountains. Sticks to himself here in camp, too. Doesn't talk much. Even has his tent way across the lake."

I was mulling this over when a familiar voice interrupted my thoughts. "Hiya, Stevie! Whatzat? Whatcha eating? Can I sit here? No one's sitting here, right? Lotsa room, right? Look what I got."

Alexander! Squishing himself in between me and Jesse, he put two plates on the table. One had a small piece of lasagna on it and a few sprigs of green salad. The other held a piece of chocolate cake the size of a small shoebox.

"Is that all for *you?*" Jesse stared, bug-eyed, at the cake.

"Yup," said Alexander, digging in. I looked around for Milly, but she was busy in the kitchen.

"Lasagna first!" I tried to sound firm but pleasant — like the girls in the baby-sitting books. "Cake later!"

"Oh, that's okay, Stevie. I can eat them both at the same time. Watch!" He swallowed the bite of cake and then stuck the fork — still covered in chocolate icing — into the lasagna. "See? First I eat a bite of cake, then I eat a bite of lasagna, then I eat a bite of cake, then —"

Now, I'm not picky about food. But this was too gross even for *me*. I headed for the dessert table. With a bit of luck, he'd be finished by the time I got back. When I returned, I stuck a big serving of apple cobbler covered in whipped cream in front of Jesse, who was watching Alexander shove a forkful of chocolate-covered lasagna into his mouth. Jesse's top lip was curled up so far you could see his gums.

"Uh, no thanks, Stevie," he said, putting a hand over his stomach. "I'm not feeling all that, uh, hungry."

I grunted. There was no way Alexander was going to make *me* miss dessert. Ignoring the layer of tomato sauce, chocolate icing and milk that was oozing across our end of the table, I dug in. Max was the first planter out of the tent.

Just as I stuck the last, delicious mouthful of apple cobbler in my mouth, Milly came marching up with a grumpy look on her face. Good! *She* could tell Alexander to eat like a human being!

"Alexander," she said, "this really is the limit! How many times have I told you to clean up your messes?"

Jesse, Alexander and I all glanced down at the table. "I'll clean it up," said Alexander, dragging his sleeve through the tomato sauce and icing. "Look! It's almost gone!"

"Not *that* mess, Alex!" Milly swabbed away at his greasy sleeve with her apron, shaking her head. "I was talking about our trailer! That's our *home* now, Alexander! I've told you over and over that you have to clean up after yourself when you play in there."

"I did!" Alexander spluttered. "I mean I didn't! I mean —"

"Never mind making excuses! As soon as I finish up in the kitchen, I'm taking you back to the trailer, and you're going to clean up every bit of that mess. Do you understand?"

Alexander kind of shrivelled up in his chair — more like a two-year-old than a five-year-old. In spite of everything, I felt sorry for him. Getting in trouble for making a mess is something I happen to be very familiar with.

"Yes, Mommy," he whispered.

Suddenly I had a brainwave. "Jesse and I can take him over to your trailer."

Milly looked surprised. Jesse looked flabbergasted.

"Are you sure?" Milly asked.

"No problem," I told her cheerfully. "We'll help him clean up." I could hardly wait. It was the perfect opportunity to get Alexander alone and question him.

"Well," said Milly, "if you really want to." She hurried back to the kitchen.

Alexander didn't move for a second. Then he covered his eyes with one arm and put his head down on the table. From the way his shoulders moved up and down, we could tell he was crying.

"Hey, don't worry," I heard myself saying. "It happens to me all the time. I'm always getting in trouble over the messes I make, aren't I, Jesse?"

"Right!" said Jesse enthusiastically. "All the time! Stevie's a real slob."

Alexander's head shot up. His face was stained with tears. "But I cleaned up all my stuff from this morning," he insisted. "My cars and my train set and my plastic animals. I cleaned up every single bit!"

Suddenly, he threw his arms around my waist and sobbed into my stomach. "I didn't do it, Stevie! It's somebody else! Somebody else keeps messing up our trailer!"

CHAPTER

"SOMEBODY ELSE? ALEXANDER, WHAT DO YOU MEAN?"

"It happened before," he said. "Mommy asked me to clean up my stuff, and I did! And then somebody messed it all up again."

Jesse and I stared at each other. A little prickle ran up the back of my neck. I grabbed Alexander by both shoulders. "Are you absolutely, positively *sure* you cleaned up your stuff today?"

"I did, Stevie! I did! Right before you and Jesse showed up!" His eyes bugged out over the tops of his glasses. I stared into them. Was he *imagining* that he'd cleaned up? Was this one of his dumb games? Was he just plain fibbing?

It was as if he could read my mind. "Rat's honour, Stevie! I would never, ever, *ever* lie to a member of the Ralph the Robot Rat Spy Club." He gave me the rat's nose salute. "Snick, snick, booga, booga —"

"Okay, okay," I said, "let's check it out. Where's your trailer?"

It was getting dark as the three of us left the cook tent. Huge evergreens rose above us, ringing the clearing like tall black towers. Scattered through the woods, tiny lights glowed where lamps had been lit in tents or campers. The clearing was still and quiet and empty — tree planters go to sleep early. The only sound was water hitting plastic curtains as someone took a last lonely shower.

"Sure gets dark quick out here in the Wilderness, doesn't it?" Jesse's voice had a little quaver in it. He jerked his head around, peering into the bushes.

"Let's go," I said. "Alexander, you lead the way." Taking my hand, he led me towards a dark patch in the trees — a narrow path leading into the bush. His hand felt small, warm and sticky. Jesse was following so closely I could feel his breath on my neck. When some leaves rustled close to our feet, he grabbed at my free hand.

"What was that?"

"It's leaves, Jesse. Quit mashing my hand."

The leaves rustled again.

"What was that?" This time, he grabbed my arm. One more rustle, and he'd be up on my shoulders.

"Probably a squirrel," I said.

"Probably a bear!" he muttered back. It was going to take a while for Jesse to get used to being in the woods.

With Alexander pulling on one hand and Jesse hanging on to the other arm, I moved sideways like a crab along the path, stumbling over roots and getting slapped in the face by branches.

Finally we reached a clearing. A small trailer looked pale and lonely in the twilight.

Alexander opened the door. "I'll put the light on."

Suddenly we were all blinking in the brightness. Alexander let out a wail. "I didn't do it!" he cried. "I didn't! I never did!"

Kids' stuff was strewn from one end of the trailer to the other. Dozens of tiny cars and trucks, pieces of wooden train, crayons, playing cards, socks, comic books — all over the beds, across the counters, in the sink, covering the floor. I'm not exactly the neatest person in the world, but even *I* had never made a mess as spectacular as this!

"Wow!" said Jesse, gazing around in shock. "Nice work, Alexander!"

"I didn't!" shrieked Alexander. His face was starting to turn purple. "I didn't, didn't, didn't, didn't, didn't —"

"It's okay," I said, patting his shoulder. I frowned at Jesse. How were we going to find out anything if our prize witness was hysterical? "We'll help you clean it up."

Alexander gave me another boa-constrictor hug. I patted his back and said "It's okay" several thousand times. The girls in the baby-sitting books would have been proud of me.

"Why don't you start at that end, Jesse? Alexander, you can pick up those Killer Cats under the table." I started gathering up a bunch of cars and trucks near the door. The sooner we got this done, the sooner I could question Alexander.

A minute later, Alexander crawled out from under the table. "Look!" he said, holding something up for me to see. It was a metal figure of Ralph the Robot Rat. Actually, it was more like an ex-Ralph. The nose had been knocked off, and one of the legs was missing. Alexander's face drooped. "See? I would never, ever, ever do this to Ralph."

Seeing that look on his face, I knew he was telling the truth. Alexander would never wreck his own Ralph the Robot Rat.

Quick as a flash, my mind leaped to the only logical conclusion. Rubberface Ragnall! Was it possible? Here? Today? In camp?

I glanced over at Jesse. "Are you thinking what I'm thinking?"

He nodded. "You bet I am," he said. "A bear!"

"A *what?*"

He gestured around the room. "It's obvious, isn't it? I mean, here we are — way out in the middle of the Wilderness. Somehow a bear got in and went on a wild rampage and —"

I sighed. "Jesse, if a bear had gotten in here today, it would look a *lot* worse than this. For starters, that door would probably be ripped right off its hinges."

Jesse stared at the door. Like most trailer doors, it looked pretty flimsy. "Off its hinges?" he said in a squeaky voice.

"Sure. Bears are really powerful. The cushions would be sliced to ribbons, the cupboards would be all bashed in, the windows would be knocked right out of their frames, and the —"

"Okay, okay. That's enough. What do *you* think happened?"

I put a finger over my lips and pointed at Alexander. He was under the table, making growling noises as he played with his Killer Cats. "I'll tell you later," I whispered. "Let's finish the clean-up first. I want to ask Alexander a few questions about the case."

"*What* case?" said Jesse.

"What *bear?*" I said right back.

It was the fastest clean-up three kids ever did. Well, two kids actually — Alexander was pretty poky. But Jesse worked really hard, glancing at the door from time to time as if he expected something large and furry to come through it. Ten minutes later, we were all sitting together around the table. Time to quiz the kid!

"Okay, Alexander," I said, "we're going to play a little game."

"Oh goody," he said, bouncing up and down in his seat. "I love games. What's it called?"

"It's called, uh, Twenty Questions. I ask you questions, and you answer them."

"Oh goody. What's question number one?"

"Remember that day you saw Rubberface — I mean, Mr. Patchouli — running away from your house? What did he look like?"

"I told you, Stevie. He was wearing a red raincoat — with a big hood."

"Did you see his face?"

"Is this question number two?"

"Yeah, sure, question number two. Did you?"

"Did I what?"

I groaned. "Did you see his *face?*"

"No, I didn't. This is easy, Stevie. I like this game."

"Did you see anything else? Like his shoes or pants or anything?"

"No. Just his raincoat."

"How big was he?"

"I dunno," said Alexander. "Grown-up size."

"There's lots of different sizes of grown-ups, Alexander. Take Jesse and me, for example. We're grown-up size. But we're still *small* grown-up size. Jesse, stand up." He stood beside me. I'm a bit taller, but we're both just over five feet. "Was Mr. Patchouli as big as Jesse and me?"

Alexander looked us over. "Way bigger than you guys!"

"Big as Stevie's dad?" asked Jesse. My dad is six feet and a bit.

Alexander nodded. "Yup," he said. "Big, like Stevie's dad. What question is this? Five? Six? Do I get a prize?"

"Sure, sure," I said absent-mindedly. "Listen, Alexander, did you hear Mr. Patchouli's voice on the phone? When he called from Hong Kong?"

"Nope," said Alexander. "What's the prize?"

I didn't answer. I was too busy thinking over what I'd found out — practically nothing. Only that Rubberface was big and wore a red raincoat. I was sure there must be other important questions I should be asking, but I couldn't think of them. Rats! What would Hercule Poirot ask if he were here? I needed to talk privately with Jesse.

Alexander was tugging on my arm. "Game's over," I told him.

"Hey," he hollered. "Wait a minute!" His lower lip stuck way out. "Where's my prize?"

Jesse shook his head. Uh-oh — Bad Baby-sitter again. He pulled something out of his pocket. "Here you go, Alex," he said. "You answered the questions really well."

"Oh, wow! A Ralph the Robot Rat ring!" Alexander stuck it on a grubby finger. "It's too big, Jesse."

"We'll put tape on the back tomorrow to make it fit."

When the door opened behind us, Jesse jumped. "Look, Mom!" said Alexander, holding out his finger. "Jesse gave me a ring."

"Well, now, isn't that nice?" Milly looked around with a smile. "My goodness, what a job you've done on this place! You're lucky to have such good friends, Alexander."

Jesse and I smiled and shrugged. "Gotta go now," I said. "Good night, Alexander."

"G' night, Steevee-Peevee," he giggled. "G' night, Jessee-Pessee! See you tomorrow!"

Steevee-Peevee . . . aghh! I gritted my teeth. As I headed out the door, I wondered, was I really going to be able to fake it as a baby-sitter long enough to solve this case?

I waited till Jesse and I were halfway down the path. "Listen," I whispered, "that wasn't any bear that made that mess. It was a human being! Somebody went into Milly and Alexander's trailer today to *search* for something."

"You mean" — I watched as the idea slowly penetrated his brain — "Rubberface Ragnall?"

"Exactly!" *Finally* he had figured it out. "Rubberface searched Milly's trailer today the same way he searched her house in Vancouver."

"Gosh!" said Jesse. "But that's impossible! I mean, we're way out here in the Wilderness. You can hear a car engine from miles away. Wouldn't somebody *notice* if a stranger came sneaking around?"

"Yes."

"Yes?"

"You're right. It would be almost impossible for a stranger to sneak in here. Especially in broad daylight."

"So?"

"So he's not a stranger."

"What?" Jesse gasped.

"Rubberface Ragnall isn't a stranger," I repeated. "He's one of the crew." Saying it out loud, I felt a chill come over me. "Think about it. It's the only possibility."

"Gosh, Stevie." Jesse glanced nervously into the trees. I didn't know who he was watching for now — a bear or Rubberface Ragnall. "We'd better tell Milly — and your dad — and —"

"No," I said. "We can't."

"Why not?"

"All we have is Alexander's word that he didn't make the mess. Did adults ever believe *you* when you were five years old and said you didn't make a mess?"

There was a silence. Then, "I see what you mean."

"Besides, what if we're wrong? What if this *is* just all Alexander's imagination?"

Jesse thought about this for a minute. "We'll look like idiots?"

"Prize idiots," I agreed.

"So what do you think we should do, Stevie? And could we keep walking, please? I don't think it's — you know — safe, standing out here in the dark like this." Jesse shuffled slowly away from me. A tree branch crackled behind him in the wind.

"Okay," I said. "Here's the plan. We're going to figure it out — you and me, Diamond & Kulniki. As soon as we find out who Rubberface Ragnall is, we'll tell my dad — and the police. The way I see it, the first thing we have to do is investigate the tree planters and —"

"Investigate the tree planters? There must be twenty or thirty of them!"

"Thirty-six."

"Thirty-six suspects!" He groaned. "That's impossible. It'll take weeks."

"No, listen. I already figured it out. We don't have to investigate them all. Most of the tree planters couldn't possibly be Rubberface."

"Why not?"

"Because my dad hired them ages ago. They phoned up for jobs last fall and got hired way back then, months before all this stuff happened to Milly in Vancouver."

"I see what you mean," said Jesse slowly. "Rubberface must have *followed* Milly and Alexander to camp. He must have been hired *after* they were already here."

"Exactly! And remember what Max told us at dinner?"

Jesse grabbed my arm. "He said that your dad had just hired some extra planters. That means Ragnall must be one of the greeners who just got hired! Stevie, you're a genius!"

"Just your average, hard-working detective," I said modestly.

"So how do we find out who the new planters are?"

"Simple! We ask my dad."

"I hope he's someplace with a light on."

He was — all alone in the cook tent, still doing paperwork at one of the long tables. A supervisor at a tree-planting camp has to keep track of all the trees that all the planters have planted; most evenings my dad stayed up late, writing down numbers and adding things up. He told us to help ourselves to some ginger-snaps from a huge jar. As we ate the cookies and drank milk, we chatted about all kinds of stuff. Finally, I couldn't wait any longer.

"I hear you just hired some new planters in Revelstoke, Dad. Jesse and I were wondering . . . what are their names?"

My dad put his pen down. "Why?"

I thought fast. "Well, we're going out to watch the planters work tomorrow, right? And I, uh, thought I'd show Jesse the difference between people who've been planting for years and people who are just starting out." There! Not bad for right off the top of my head. Jesse nodded in agreement.

"Well, let's see," said my dad. "I hired three greeners last week — Lucille, Wilbur and Jake. No, four! Mountain Man, too."

Jesse and I glanced at each other. Mountain Man! I'd forgotten that he was one of the new planters.

"Thanks, Dad. The cookies are terrific. Can we take some with us?"

I grabbed Jesse's hand, and we raced back to our camper. "Quick!" I said as we ran in the door. "Find a piece of paper and a pen! Before we forget the names." We hunted through drawers and cupboards till Jesse found a notebook and an old chewed-up yellow pencil.

"Good," I said. "Make a heading at the top — LIST OF SUSPECTS."

Our list looked like this:

LIST OF SUSPECTS
1. LUCILLE
2. JAKE
3. WILBUR
4. MOUNTAIN MAN

"This is progress," said Jesse. "A while ago, we had thirty-six suspects. Now we've got it down to four."

"Three," I said, peering at the list. "Lucille is a woman's name. Rubberface Ragnall is definitely a man. Cross off Lucille."

"Oh," said Jesse. "Oh, right." He drew a thick line through Lucille's name.

"We'll have a perfect opportunity to check these guys out tomorrow," I said, "when my dad takes us to watch the tree planters. All we have to do is figure out who" — I glanced at the list — "Jake and Wilbur are. We already know who Mountain Man is."

"Yeah," said Jesse. "Unfortunately."

"Listen," I said, "someone's coming. Probably my dad." Jesse stuffed the list in his pocket. By the time my dad opened the door, we were both standing at the tiny sink, doing a very thorough job of brushing our teeth.

Ten minutes later, I was up in my loft, lying in the darkness, listening. A wilderness camp at night must be one of the quietest places in the world. Nothing but the wind shifting through the branches, the soft rustle of leaves, and tiny animals running around on their night-time business. Maybe I was imagining it, but I thought I could hear the sound of waves lapping against the shore of the lake. It was peaceful — so peaceful I could almost forget the excitement of the day.

Almost.

An owl cried out in the distance. "Hoo! Hoo! Hoo!"

"That's what I want to know," I mumbled sleepily. "Who?"

CHAPTER

WHEN I WOKE UP, IT WAS EIGHT-THIRTY. JESSE and my dad were both gone. I threw on some clothes and headed down to the cook tent. Rebecca was stacking dishes in a corner, and Milly was measuring flour into a bowl as big as a sink. A huge pile of carrots lay on the counter.

"What are you making?" I asked.

"Carrot cake. Thank goodness for the food processor — it would take me days to grate all these carrots. There's still some breakfast in the oven, if you're hungry."

I helped myself to scrambled eggs, about ten slices of bacon, French toast and a heap of hash browns. Deluxe! If I'd been at home, I would have been eating corn flakes or — if I was lucky — a toasted bagel. Food was one of the reasons I loved to visit tree-planting camps. Missing school was another. And this camp had a bonus — a real, live, genuine mystery.

As I sat down with my breakfast, Jesse strolled into the tent. Right behind him, dancing around with excitement, came . . . Alexander. He was wearing a red-and-white jacket with a big picture of Ralph the Robot Rat on the back and five or six pockets scattered across the front.

"Where you been, Stevie? We been down at the lake for hours. We caught some minnows in a plastic bag, and then I saw a frog, and then we threw some stones in the water, and then we made a fort and —"

"Alexander, please. I just woke up."

"Yeah," said Jesse, "but everyone else has been up since six. Alex and I had breakfast with the tree planters. The trucks took off at seven."

"Your daddy said he'd come back for us, Stevie," said Alexander. "He said he'd take us out to the block."

"What's a block?" asked Jesse.

"It's where the planters are working," I told him. "Block is short for cut-block. It's a part of the forest that's been logged, so the planters have to plant new trees there."

It was almost nine-thirty when my dad pulled into camp, driving a crew cab. A crew cab is this big truck that has two bench seats in the front so it can carry a bunch of people. The open part at the back is where they put the boxes of baby trees for planting. Alexander immediately jumped into the front seat with Jesse and my dad, leaving *me* to sit in the back seat all by myself.

At first, I just stared at the back of Alexander's head and fumed. But after a while, it got to be fun. We were riding on rough old logging roads, full of ruts and holes and stones and logs, and the truck bounced around all over the place. We got.

rocked from side to side and up and down, and, if we weren't wearing seat belts, our heads would probably have hit the roof.

"Who-a-o-a-o-a-o-a!" yelled Jesse, as Alexander shrieked. Their heads bobbed up and down like apples at Hallowe'en. I grabbed an arm rest as the truck dived into a pothole. Tree branches swished across the windshield. Sometimes we could see huge mountains rise up out of the trees. At other times, noisy white streams rushed alongside. For a while, the road crawled along the steep edge of a mountain. I glanced down — way, way down — and then slid over to the other side of the truck, quickly switching seat belts. No sense in having all our weight on the tippy side, right? After about half an hour, we spotted the first planters, scattered over a bare, charred area as big as a couple of football fields.

"What happened here?" Jesse asked, as my dad pulled the truck to a stop. "A forest fire?"

"Not exactly," said my dad. "This is a burn. After they logged this area, they set a fire to get rid of some of the leftover branches and tree trunks."

"Boy!" said Jesse. "Looks like the end of the world."

I could see what he meant. The whole area was full of burned and charred branches and thick black tree trunks. It looked like the leftovers of a gigantic campfire. All we could see of the planters were little dots of colour where their shirts stood out against the black.

My dad turned the truck off. "Eventually, there'll be a forest here again. That's what we're here for."

"Sure," said Jesse, "but that'll take years and years, won't it?"

"Fifty years or so."

"Fifty years!" said Jesse. "That's forever."

My dad smiled, but it wasn't a happy smile. "It *is* forever, isn't it?"

Alexander was already out of the truck. He whipped off his jacket, threw it into the front seat and headed into the burn. "Come on!" he yelled. Jesse and I followed. Within minutes, all three of us had black smears and streaks across our clothes. It was like walking through a coal pit.

"Hi, guys." It was Max. He was wearing a raggedy-looking sweatshirt and gym shorts over a pair of long underwear. Heavy hiking boots covered his feet. He had twisted a scarf up into a kind of cord and was wearing it around his forehead as a sweatband. Sounds weird, I know, but it was a pretty regular outfit for a tree planter.

"Wow!" said Alexander. "Look at all those trees." Three big canvas bags hung from a belt around Max's waist. They were full of baby trees — spruce seedlings. "How many you got in there, Max?"

"Oh, about four hundred — I just filled up. Want to follow along and watch?"

We tagged along for a while as Max planted. Even though he kept stopping every few steps to plant a tree, he moved fast, climbing over huge rocks and burned logs and branches. He had a funny-looking shovel — the metal part at the bottom was just a sharp little triangle to poke a skinny hole into the earth. He kept jabbing at the ground with it.

"Whatcha doing?" Alexander asked.

"Testing the ground," said Max. "I have to find a good spot — a place where the tree has a chance to grow." He must have found one because he jammed his shovel hard into the ground and wiggled it back and forth to make a hole. Grabbing a baby tree, he stuck its root ball into the hole and then kicked dirt into the hole.

He moved on, and we scrambled to keep up, Alexander in the lead. I had expected him to get left behind and start whining, but he wasn't even breathing hard.

"How many trees do you plant in a day, Max?" asked Jesse.

"On a good day, maybe a thousand," said Max, planting another seedling.

"A thousand trees! In just one day?" But Max was already three or four metres ahead of us.

"Max is a highballer," I told Jesse.

"What's that?"

"Kind of the opposite of a greener. Someone who's been planting for a long time — someone who's really good at it."

"Gosh," said Jesse. "A thousand trees. That's practically a forest."

"It would be," I said, "if they all lived. But they don't." I'd learned this from my dad.

"How many trees does a greener plant in a day?"

"Probably just a few hundred," I said, slowing to a stop. "Planters get paid for each tree they plant, so the greeners don't make as much money. Speaking of greeners — hey, Alexander! Can you show us who Wilbur is? And Jake?"

"Sure!" He looked around, then pointed. "That's Wilbur over there — with Lucille."

I followed the direction of his finger. Even from a distance, I could tell that Lucille and Wilbur weren't nearly as good at planting trees as Max. They were moving slowly and took longer to find a good place for a seedling. As we got closer, I could see this confused look on Wilbur's face — as if he couldn't exactly figure out what he was doing — and he was definitely panting. He was on the chubby side with a round face, big pouchy cheeks and he was starting to go bald on top. His glasses were all steamed up. As we came close, he stopped to wipe the sweat off his forehead.

"Oooohhhh," he moaned, as he sat down on a blackened piece of log. "My back is killing me. Hi, kids!" He peered at me. "You must be Mike's daughter."

"Yup!" I said. "I'm Stevie, and this is my part — I mean, my friend, Jesse."

"Pleased to meet you — both of you," said Wilbur. He pulled a package of cigarettes out of his pocket and lit one. "Hey! Lucille! Take a break. Say hi to the kids."

Lucille stopped and jabbed her shovel into the ground. She was tall and strong looking with wide shoulders and smooth, muscled arms. Her hair was short and so light that it was almost white — what we could see of it underneath her scarf.

"I've got no time for breaks. Or kids, either. Not if I'm going to make any money today." She stared at us with eyes that were the pale blue colour of the sky on a hot day. Then she trudged on.

Wilbur stood up slowly, rubbing his back. "Don't mind Lucille. She's just having a bad day." Stubbing out his cigarette, he hurried to catch up with her. As the two of them slowly picked their way over the burn, Lucille stayed ahead, stopping every now and then until Wilbur caught up. She wasn't a terrific planter, but she was doing way better than he was. Jesse started to follow, but I shook my head.

"Lucille seems to be a little crabby," I said.

"Wanna see Jake?" asked Alexander. "He's over there." He pointed at a tall planter with long black hair flowing down his back in curly waves. He was heading towards the trucks. Five or six planters were gathered there, putting seedlings into their bags and filling their water bottles from a big cooler. Jesse, Alexander and I followed. As we came close, Alexander called out. "Hey, Jake, hi! Can we watch you plant?"

Jake jumped up onto the back of one of the trucks, opened a box of baby trees and started filling his bags.

"Jake?" said Alexander again. Still no answer. The planters looked at Alexander and then at Jake. "Hey, Jake!" one of them said.

Jake finally glanced up. Wow! He looked like one of those rock stars on the music channel. Slim and athletic — the total opposite of Wilbur. He had tanned skin, a thick black moustache and white even teeth. "What?" he said.

"Alexander's talking to you," said the planter. "He wants to know if he can watch you."

"Oh," said Jake, spotting us for the first time.

"Oh sure. Just don't get in my way." Turning back to the tree boxes, he kept filling his bags.

"He didn't answer when two different people called his name," Jesse whispered. "Don't you think that's a bit suspicious?"

"Maybe," I whispered back, "but he might just be hard of hearing."

Jake finished filling his bags and headed into the burn. Alexander ran along beside him, and Jesse and I followed. Alexander was chattering away, mostly about Ralph the Robot Rat and the Spy Club, but Jake didn't pay much attention. He was striding along fast on his long legs, stopping only to stick his shovel into the ground and put a tree in behind it.

"He's a greener, too, right?" whispered Jesse. "Like Lucille and Wilbur?"

"Right," I said, "but he's doing way better than they are."

We followed Jake all the way across the burn into an open area filled with tall grass. It was hard, dirty work, crawling over all those logs and rocks and stumps, and the sun beat down as if it were the middle of summer. Jake didn't say a word, and I was panting too hard to ask questions.

Just as I was wondering if this really *was* the best way to investigate our suspects, my dad called out from across the grassy area.

"Hey! You guys interested in a quad ride?"

"Yippee!" yelled Alexander.

"A *what* ride?" asked Jesse.

I pointed at a funny-looking vehicle parked

behind my dad. It was kind of like a motorcycle, except that it had four big fat puffy wheels. We ran over.

"Weird," said Jesse. "What is it?"

"It's an all-terrain vehicle," my dad explained. "It's called a quad, and it can go practically anywhere — through streams, over fields — places where there are no roads. Who's first for a ride?"

Alexander, of course, was already sitting on the quad. My dad climbed on behind him. "Let's go, Alex. I'll be back for you guys later." They roared off into some scrubby trees. We could hear Alexander yelling "Wheeeeeeee!" as they disappeared.

Jesse looked around to see where Jake was — almost out of sight — before he spoke. "So what do you think, Stevie? How come Jake doesn't answer when people say his name?"

"There are only two possibilities that I can think of," I said slowly. "One — he's hard of hearing. And two — his name's not really Jake."

"You mean, like maybe it's . . . Rubberface Ragnall?" said Jesse.

"Maybe," I said, thinking hard. "The question is, how do we find out?"

"I know!" said Jesse. "We can test his hearing. We sneak up on him and burst a paper bag filled with air right behind his head. It'll make a huge bang. If he doesn't turn around, he's hard of hearing!"

Sounded good to me. "Okay, we'll do it. Later."

"Look!" said Jesse. "Up there!" He grabbed his

binoculars and pointed them into the sky. "An eagle! No, two of them!"

The birds were just specks to me. But after Jesse had had a chance to watch for a while, he handed me the binoculars, and I could see heads and wings and sharp curved beaks as the eagles swooped and soared.

"Must be looking for food," said Jesse, glancing around the meadow. "There's probably a whole bunch of field mice around here." We took turns watching until we heard the quad coming back.

Alexander was still hollering "Wheeeeeee!" as my dad stopped in front of us. Jesse got a ride next, and ten minutes later it was my turn. It was great — we tore across the meadow, bouncing over little rocks and bumps and whipping past skinny trees. I hung on tight to my dad's waist, and my hair flew out behind me in the wind. When we came to a tiny stream, we just roared straight through, the water splashing up over our feet and legs. "Wheeeeeee!" I yelled, just like Alexander.

When we got back, Jesse wanted to have a closer look at the quad. He sat on it and ran his hands over the controls. "How do you start it? How does it work?"

Alexander was down on his hands and knees in a second. "Like this," he said. "There's this little thing down here, see? By your foot? And you have to lift it up with your toe before you turn the key on. Then you put your hand over here, see?" He pointed to a fat part of the handlebar. "And you turn it like this. Then you pull up the thing again with your toe. That gets you into first gear, see?"

"How do *you* know all that?" I stared at Alexander. "You're only in kindergarten!"

My dad laughed. "Alexander's pretty amazing. Every time a truck breaks down, he hangs around, giving advice to whoever's working on it. Milly says he's been nuts about cars and trucks ever since he was two."

"I've got a whole collection," said Alexander. "A zillion cars and trucks and three trains — one's electric. Mommy says I'm a mechanical genius. Sort of like that guy Mozart."

"Mozart?" I repeated. "A mechanical genius?"

"No, Stevie — you silly!" He laughed so long I finally had to hit him on the back. "Mozart was a *musical* genius! But we're both sort of prod . . . prod —"

"Prodigies," said my dad. "A prodigy is a child who is brilliant at some particular talent."

Hmph, I thought. Jesse and I were brilliant at detecting. How come nobody ever called *us* prodigies? I'd have to remember to write the word down as soon as I got back to camp. Prodigies, prodigies, prodigies — maybe we could add it to our business cards. Stevie Diamond and Jesse Kulniki, Detective Prodigies.

VRRRRMMM! "Hey!" yelled Jesse. "Look! I started the quad! Stevie, I started it!"

My dad climbed on behind Jesse and helped him drive in slow circles around the meadow. Then I tried, and then Alexander had a turn. It was fun, but I really wanted to gun it full speed across that stream — as fast as it would go and *without* my dad.

"Time to head back to camp, guys," said my dad finally. "I've still got a lot of work to do today."

Back in the crew cab, Alexander started searching the seats. "Hey! Where's my jacket?"

"Did you lose it?" I asked. "What did it look like?"

"Red and white." Alexander looked panicky. "Stevie, it was my special Ralph the Robot Rat jacket."

"Don't worry. We'll find it." But we didn't. Jesse and my dad checked both seats of the crew cab and the back of the truck, too. We even looked around outside near the water cooler and tree boxes.

"Are you sure you didn't leave it out on the block?" my dad asked.

"I didn't!" said Alexander. "I took it off and left it right here. Remember, Stevie?"

Actually, no, I didn't. "It'll turn up," I said. "Someone will find it and bring it back to camp." Alexander didn't look convinced. His face got all quivery, but he didn't cry — not then and not on the whole drive back to camp. It wasn't nearly as much fun as the ride out.

"Maybe it was a bear," mumbled Jesse. "Maybe a bear snuck up and — you know — thought it was a sandwich or something."

I rolled my eyes. "Right. A bear ate Alexander's jacket."

"I don't mean *ate* it. Just — you know — dragged it off. Back to its — what do you call it — nest or whatever it is!"

I shook my head. My dad tried not to smile. Alexander forgot about his jacket and laughed out loud. Even *he* knew more about the wilderness than Jesse.

Dinner was as delicious as the night before — fried chicken, baked potatoes with sour cream, vegetable-cheese casserole for the vegetarians, two kinds of salad and scrumptious desserts — carrot cake, mocha mousse and giant chocolate-chip cookies. Jesse and I ate as fast as we could. We had decided to test Jake's hearing right after dinner in the cook tent.

Jake was sitting at a table with some other planters, who were all talking about how many trees they'd planted that day. Jake joined in sometimes, but mostly he just ate his dinner and stared off into space.

"Now?" said Jesse as we carried our plates over to the stacking area.

"Now!" I said. "Where's the bag?" We had tossed a coin to see who would burst it behind Jake's head. I lost.

I felt a little nervous about this bag thing, but I couldn't think of another way to find out if Jake really *was* hard of hearing. A good detective, I figured, has to take a few risks. I pulled out the paper bag we had gotten from the kitchen. Holding the opening almost shut, I blew into it. It swelled up with air, like a balloon.

"Ready?" asked Jesse with a gulp.

"Ready!" I held the paper bag behind my back.

We took a deep breath and walked towards the table where Jake sat with his back to us. His long dark hair gleamed under the hanging light bulb. A planter sitting across from him glanced up at us and waved. For just a second, I slowed down. What if Jake got mad? What if he flipped right out? What if — ???

"Stevie!" Jesse hissed. "Come on."

Easy for you, I thought. You don't have to burst the bag.

Still, he was right. I took another deep breath and marched up behind Jake. Swinging the bag around in front of me, I held it right behind his head and smashed it with both hands.

POW! It sounded as if a cannon had been shot off!

For just a second, Jake's head rose in the air. Then suddenly it was gone. In fact, all of him was gone. Where was he? Jesse and I stared at each other. The other planters just sat there with their mouths hanging open. Finally, one of them said, in a strangled voice, "Jake?"

I looked down. There he was, crouched under the table. His eyes were as big as doughnuts.

Jesse whispered, "I think his hearing is, uh, pretty good."

My dad came running up. "Stevie! What on earth is going on here? Jake! Are you okay?" He helped Jake climb out from under the table. Jake was shaking his head and rubbing his hands against his ears.

My dad stared at the shredded paper bag in my hand. "Okay," he said in a slow, calm, this-means-trouble voice. "Maybe you'd like to explain this, Stevie?"

"I, uh, I . . . " Suddenly, the whole thing seemed like a really dumb idea.

"Do you know what a dumb idea that was?" said my dad. "Haven't I told you never to make a loud noise right beside someone's ear? You could have damaged Jake's hearing — permanently!"

"Yes, Dad," I said. Now I remembered — he *had* told me. But he'd been talking about yelling, not about paper bags.

"Sorry," I said. "Sorry, Jake. Sorry, Dad."

"Sorry. Sorry, too," said Jesse. Good old Jesse — sharing the blame even when he didn't have to.

"You two come with me," said my dad. As we followed him to another table, I knew we were in for the big lecture. Actually, we got three. First we got the big lecture on ears and hearing and burst eardrums and dumb practical jokes. Then we got the big lecture on being guests in camp and being responsible and not causing trouble. Finally, we got the big lecture on the consequences of our behaviour — namely, that if we pulled something like this again, maybe we'd get sent back to the city.

"Okay, Dad," I said. "We got it. We'll smarten up."

"Right," said Jesse, nodding rapidly. "Me too. Smarten right up. Mr. Diamond. Sir!"

We slunk out of the cook tent and headed down the main path. As we passed a couple of campsites, planters waved or called out hi to us. At a large blue tent, we spotted Wilbur and Lucille having a conversation, their heads almost touching. I strained my ears to hear, but their voices were too low to make anything out. After a minute, Wilbur disappeared into his tent. Lucille turned and headed in our direction. She had a huge pair of binoculars around her neck and a flashlight in her hand. I guess she wasn't really looking where she was going because she almost ran us down.

"What the —" She stopped and drew her breath in sharply. "What are you two doing here? Eavesdropping?"

"No way," I said. "We didn't hear a word." That, at least, was the truth. But why was she so upset about us listening?

"Go on back to your camper. Right now. Go to bed." She made a shooing motion with her hands, as if we were a couple of dogs. Jesse and I didn't budge. Shaking her head, she walked away — straight into the forest. She turned and made a final shooing gesture at us. Then, with a "Tsk!" sound, she disappeared into the woods.

"Now what got into her?" asked Jesse. "And where the heck is she going? There are no tents or campers in there, are there, Stevie?"

"No," I said, puzzled. "Nothing. Not even a path."

We watched, but she didn't come out again.

"She had binoculars," I said. "Now why would she —"

"Stevie! Jesse! Look! I got it back." Alexander was racing towards us, waving his jacket. "Colleen found it. It was just lying out there on the block. I'm so happy, I could just kiss it!" And he did, too. He actually scrunched up his jacket and kissed it.

"That's great, Alexander," said Jesse. "I'm happy for you."

Wait a minute. "What happened to the pockets?" I asked. Every one of the pockets — all six of them — had been pulled inside out. "Did you do this, Alexander?"

He shook his head. "That's how it was when Colleen found it. She asked me how come I pulled all the pockets out. But I didn't, Stevie. I never did."

Then I noticed the lining. It was ripped — or cut — along the bottom. There was room to stick your hand right inside. "Did you do this?" I asked. "Was it ripped like this before?"

Alexander stared. "No!" he said. "My mommy always sews my stuff up as soon as it gets ripped. How did *that* happen?"

I shook my head, trying to figure it out. Looking down, I ran my hand over the front of the jacket, touching the pockets, one by one. They puffed out softly like fat white mushrooms. Carefully, I felt along the shredded edge of the jacket lining. Then I handed the jacket back to Alexander. He ran off to show the rip to his mom.

"Guess he lost it when we were following the planters today," said Jesse.

I shook my head. "He didn't lose it."

"What do you mean?"

"Just that. Alexander didn't *lose* his jacket today. It was *stolen*. And then it was searched. Even the lining — did you see how it was slit open?"

Jesse and I stared at each other as we both realized what I was saying.

"That means," said Jesse, "that Rubberface Ragnall *was* out there on the block today. We . . . we might have been standing right beside him."

I nodded. "We might have been following him!"

CHAPTER

6

THE NEXT DAY WAS A DAY OFF WORK FOR THE tree planters. I knew from other visits that most of them would spend the day just hanging around camp and resting up. When my dad went down to breakfast, Jesse and I stayed behind in the camper. We needed to do some planning, and I didn't see how we could do it with a certain five-year-old kid listening in.

"Let's start with the suspect list," I said. "We need to add the stuff we found out yesterday."

After a few minutes of searching, Jesse finally found the list in the pocket of his pants from the day before. Being such an organized guy, he had already stashed the pants in his laundry bag. The paper was a little crumpled, but we pressed it out straight. A few minutes later, it looked like this.

LIST OF SUSPECTS
1. ~~LUCILLE~~
2. JAKE — DOESN'T ANSWER TO NAME
3. WILBUR — HANGS OUT WITH GROUCHY CHARACTER (LUCILLE)
4. MOUNTAIN MAN — VERY CREEPY

"We're on the right track, Stevie. All three of our suspects were planting on the block yesterday. They *all* had a chance to snatch the jacket."

"Mountain Man, too?"

Jesse nodded. "I spotted him just before we drove away."

"You did? How come you didn't tell me?"

Jesse looked uncomfortable. "I thought you might want to follow him around. And, uh, to tell you the truth, Stevie, I wasn't crazy about that idea."

"Hmmm," I said. "Then you'll probably be even *less* crazy about my plan for this morning."

"What plan?"

"My plan to interview the suspects. Starting with Mountain Man."

"What!!!" He looked as if I'd just suggested leaping off a cliff.

"Listen, Jesse, we can't just ignore the scary suspects. What kind of detective would do that? Besides, we'll go undercover."

"You mean in disguise?" He looked relieved. "What will our cover be?"

"We'll pretend to be a couple of kids visiting his campsite. It'll give us a chance to snoop around."

"What do you mean, *pretend* to be kids? We *are* kids."

"Exactly! That's why it's so perfect! Nobody would ever expect a couple of twelve-year-old kids to be experienced detectives. All we have to do is look like ourselves and act innocent and dumb."

"Innocent and dumb? Gosh, I don't know, Stevie. I'm not much of an actor."

"You'll do fine. I have faith in you. Now let's get some breakfast."

Most of the planters were still sitting around the cook tent, drinking coffee and talking. Wilbur and Lucille were playing double solitaire. Jesse and I watched for a few minutes, but you can't detect much from a silent card game. Lucille wasn't wearing a scarf today, and her blond hair looked like straw. She glanced over at me a couple of times without smiling. Those pale blue eyes made me feel all prickly — as if I'd rubbed up against a cactus.

We wandered over to where Max was showing some postcards to Colleen and Rebecca. I asked in my most casual voice about Mountain Man. Nobody was sure, but Rebecca figured he'd driven into town with a couple of other planters. Jesse's mouth curled into a smile of relief.

"Forget it," I whispered. "We're still going to his campsite."

We were just helping ourselves to pancakes, fruit salad and yogurt — and for me, sausages — when Alexander popped up behind us. "There you are! I been waiting and waiting and *waiting* to have breakfast with you guys! Wow! Ever yummy!"

Breakfast *did* look yummy. But that was before Alexander turned his meal into a giant mush pile. Ketchup smeared on the pancakes, strawberry syrup all over the sausages — uggh! Jesse and I gobbled down our food and tried not to look.

When we stood up from the table with our dishes, Alexander jumped up, too. "Where we going, guys?"

Now what? How could Jesse and I do any investigating with Alexander along? Then I remembered — Mountain Man's campsite was over on the other side of Ruby Lake. Jesse and I could *canoe* over there! I was pretty sure Milly wouldn't let Alexander come with us in a canoe.

I was right.

"I *know* you've been taking swimming lessons, Alexander, and I *know* you'd sit still in the middle of the canoe and not make a peep. But I just can't let you go out alone with Stevie and Jesse." Milly was firm. "Wait till this afternoon, and I'll take you for a ride myself."

"But Mommeeeeeeee —"

I almost felt sorry for Alexander. I said, *almost*. He followed us down to the lake and moped around while we put on our life jackets and flipped a canoe into the water. It was a terrific morning for canoeing — sunny and warm. No wind at all, and the lake was as flat as the pancakes we'd just eaten. The water was icy on my bare feet as I walked the canoe out past the shallows, and so clear you could see the tiny coloured stones on the bottom.

Jesse, meanwhile, was watching me. It was his very first time in a canoe, and I guess he figured the best thing to do would be to copy every single move I made. It made things a bit difficult when we climbed in.

"Uh, no, Jesse, one of us has to go in the *front*. See? That seat up there?"

"Oh! Oh sure. Sorry, Stevie." He stood up and started walking down the spine of the canoe.

"NO!" I hollered. "NO! Don't stand up! Don't ever —"

"Aaaaaaaaaaaaaaaa —"

The canoe jerked wildly from side to side. I grabbed on to the sides and held on. An arm flew up, then a leg, then — SPLASH!

"Rule number one," I said, when Jesse's head finally appeared above the water. "Never stand up in a canoe."

Alexander was leaping around with delight on shore. "Do it again, Jesse! Do it again!"

Jesse went back to the camper to get changed, which gave Alexander a chance to fill me in on this car he was designing. "It's for Ralph the Robot Rat, and I got about a billion drawings of it, Stevie. It's really neat looking, see? It's silver and kind of like a sports car except it can fly, and it's called a —"

"Let me guess. A Ratmobile, right?"

"How'd you know? Yeah! A Ratmobile."

When he'd finished describing every single gear and crank in the Ratmobile, he took a quick breath and started telling me the names of his Killer Cats.

"There's Claude the Claw, see? And he's best friends with Francis the Fang, see? But they're not nearly as bad as this big humungous guy named One-Eyed Willy. Wanna know how One-Eyed Willy lost his eye?"

"No."

"Well, it was like this, see —"

On our second try, I gave Jesse step-by-step directions about how to get into a canoe, and we got launched with no problem. Both of us paddled like mad, and soon the canoe was definitely moving. Trouble was, it wasn't exactly going in the direction we had in mind.

"Hey!" yelled Alexander from the shore. "How come you guys are going around in circles?"

"Yeah!" said Jesse, glancing back over his shoulder. "How come we're going in circles?"

"It's not *my* fault." I struggled to straighten out the canoe. "I've never paddled in the stern before. My dad always sits at the back and steers. Don't worry, though — I'll figure it out."

It took a while, as I experimented with a bunch of different paddling techniques, but finally, we were travelling more or less smoothly across the water. The lake was a silvery blue colour, surrounded by giant bulrushes. As we paddled, I heard the soft plop of a fish jumping nearby. Then, in the distance, an eerie cry, like the whistle of a ghost.

"What was that?" Jesse stopped, his paddle held stiff above the water.

"A loon."

"You mean, like the bird on the coin?" Lifting his binoculars, he pointed them towards the sound. I guess he couldn't spot the loon because a moment later he aimed the glasses at Mountain Man's camp.

"Looks like no one's there, Stevie."

"Good."

I kept paddling. It was tiring work. Maybe because I was paddling alone. "Jesse!" He was hunched over his belt. "What the heck are you doing?"

"Just checking our direction on my compass. We're heading — let's see — northeast."

"We don't *need* a compass!" I pointed at Mountain Man's campsite. "We can *see* where we're going."

"Yeah, I know, Stevie, but it's always a good idea to know which direction you're headed when you're out in the —"

"I know — Wilderness." I sighed.

We were close enough now to get a good look at the strange, lonely campsite on the opposite shore. Mountain Man had stretched a tarp — a big piece of blue plastic — over a frame of rough-cut branches to make a kind of homemade tent at the top of a rise. Beside it was a circle of charred rocks, and beside that, a pile of freshly chopped firewood. A big chunk of log stood upright nearby.

"Ulp!" said Jesse. Stuck into that log was the biggest, shiniest axe I've ever seen.

"It's okay," I whispered over the slap of my paddle. "We're undercover, remember? Just a couple of friendly, innocent kids."

The truth was, that axe made *me* a little nervous, too.

The place looked deserted. No smoke rising from the firepit, no movement, no sound from the tent. We beached the canoe and stepped out onto Mountain Man's campsite.

"HALLO!" I yelled. "HALLO! Anybody home?"

"Shh, Stevie! What are you *doing?*"

"What do you think I'm doing? Letting him know we're here. Do you want to surprise him or something?"

"Oh," said Jesse. "I guess not. HALLO, MOUNTAIN MAN! IT'S JUST US — STEVIE AND JESSE! JUST A COUPLE OF KIDS COME TO VISIT!"

We walked slowly up the hill from the shore, yelling and stomping our feet. "Mountain Man!" I hollered. "Are you there?"

Finally, we were standing outside the tent. Jesse's right hand gripped my left so tightly I could feel bones crunch. He raised his left hand and rapped against one of the poles holding up the tarp.

"Knock, knock?" he said in a quavery voice. "Anybody home?"

We waited. Then, behind us — a sudden shuffling noise! We whirled in time to see a squirrel skittering into the trees.

It took at least a minute for my heart to slow down again. "Mountain Man's not here. He must have gone into town, like Rebecca said."

I remembered something else. "There's no canoe here, either, except the one we brought. If Mountain Man were here, there'd be another canoe."

Jesse's voice was still nervous. "Are you sure?"

"Sure I'm sure. Watch!" I stuck my head inside the tent. "HEY, MOUNTAIN MAN, YOU UGLY OLD RATBAG OF A WEASEL! WAKIE, WAKIE! RISE AND SHINE!"

Silence. "See, Jesse? No one home."

We stepped inside and looked around. What a mess! Piles of dirty clothes everywhere plus two or three big duffel bags full of who knew what? Over in the corner was a camp cot with sleeping bags, pillows and blankets heaped on it. Beside it was a kind of table made out of two pieces of log and a board. It held a half-burned white candle stuck to an upside-down jar lid. Underneath the cot was a battered old briefcase. A pile of newspapers was stacked in a wooden crate at the far end. Two tree-planting shovels were propped up beside the crate, and a couple of enormous black work boots lay on their sides with their tongues hanging out like ugly old dogs'. Except for the sound of our breathing, the place was silent.

"You're right, Stevie." Jesse's voice startled me. "There's no one home. Let's get out of here!" He had one foot already out the door.

"Are you kidding? This is a perfect opportunity to search the place."

"Awww, Stevie, that guy's a real weirdo. Even the other planters don't talk to him. What if he comes back? What if he catches us here?"

"Will you please relax? If he comes back, we'll be able to see him coming long before he gets here. Do you see any canoes on the lake?"

He looked. "Well . . . no."

"Then we're safe. Come on. You look through those duffel bags over there. I'm going to check out the briefcase."

I hauled it out from under the cot. It was covered in dust and kind of bashed up and — rats! — it had a combination lock on it.

"Stevie?"

"Yeah?"

"I was just wondering. Do you, uh, think there are any bears over on this side of the lake?"

I gave him a look. "Okay," he said quickly. "Just asking!"

I started to fiddle with the lock. How on earth was I going to get it open? I stared at it gloomily. There must be something really important inside. I fiddled some more. Then I shook it. Finally I banged my fist down hard on the lid.

Click! The briefcase popped open. Must have been unlocked all along.

It was jammed with books and papers. Little skinny funny-looking books with cloth and plastic covers. Long, almost transparent papers covered in writing. I shuffled through the papers quickly and leafed through the strange-looking books. There was just one thing they all had in common.

Every single book and paper in that briefcase was in Chinese writing!

"Jesse! Take a look at this."

He peered over my shoulder. "What is it?"

"It's Chinese. Look! Some of it's written by hand." I held up a paper to show him. You could see the ink marks where someone had formed the different characters. (I knew the letters were called characters because we'd had to make some in a school project once.)

"Stevie," said Jesse in a strange voice, "what language do they speak and write in Hong Kong?"

I had been thinking exactly the same thing. "Chinese!"

"I'm getting out of here!" He was headed for the door when I grabbed him.

"Wait! Just five more minutes, that's all! Check the lake, if you like. Please, Jesse?"

"Okay, but just five minutes, got it? After that, we leave!"

"Right!"

After taking a final look through the briefcase to make sure there was nothing written in English, I closed it and shoved it back underneath the cot. Then I glanced at the top of the cot. Big piles of pillows and a couple of sleeping bags. Maybe there was something underneath all that stuff.

I pulled off a dark blue sleeping bag. Underneath was another sleeping bag — a brown one. I pulled that back, too. Then I screamed.

A nose! A long, beaky nose. Part of a face, of course, and a body, too, but they were still covered in sleeping bag. I knew that nose. It was bony and knobby and bent in the middle. Mountain Man's nose!

The nostrils flared.

Screaming even louder, I took a huge leap backwards — and crashed into Jesse. Both of us went flying across the tent. We must have hit some of the support poles because the next thing I knew, the tent had collapsed, and I was all tangled up in huge folds of blue tarp with something hard thumping against my shoulder — Jesse's foot, I think. I could hear him yelling, and I could hear some other yelling, too, in a deeper voice. I struggled against the collapsed tent. It felt like a huge fishnet, and I felt like a fish trapped inside. A hand grabbed mine and pulled.

Whose hand?

Suddenly I was out in the sunshine, dragged out from under the tarp by — thank goodness! — Jesse.

"Run!" he yelled. Not that he needed to. I could have beat a racehorse back to the canoe. It wasn't until we were on our way with our paddles flashing that I glanced back up the hill.

The tent was a twisting, heaving, growling, snarling mass of blue plastic. Mountain Man was still trapped inside. But I knew he wouldn't be there for long. A silver glint caught my eye. The axe!

"Paddle!" I yelled. "Faster! Faster!"

We didn't say a word until we were almost across Ruby Lake. Looking back, I could see Mountain Man finally crawling out from under the tangled tarp. He stood up and looked across the lake. I scrunched down low in the canoe.

"So!" muttered Jesse in this grouchy voice. He was scrunched down, too. "So Mountain Man's gone to town, eh? So he couldn't be there without a canoe, eh?"

"There must be a path through the woods to his campsite. How was I supposed to know?"

"I *told* you we should leave. I *told* you it wasn't safe. Didn't I *tell* you?" When he scrunched low in the canoe that way, his paddle hit the water at a funny angle, sending sprays of water back in my face.

Mumble, grumble. I could hear his voice, but I couldn't make out the words.

"What did you say?"

"I said I QUIT!"

"What??" Pulling my paddle out of the water, I stared at his hunched-over back. "You *can't* quit! What about our partnership? What about our business cards? What about our case?"

"Case, shmase!" he sputtered. "We barely got away just now, Stevie. What if Mountain Man had caught us? And what about yesterday with Jake and the paper bag? What kind of dumb idea was that?"

"That was *your* idea."

"I don't care whose idea it was. It's dumb! I quit!"

The canoe hit the bank with a thud. Jesse began to rise from his seat. "Wait!" I said. "Rule number one. Don't st —"

But with a last dirty look at me, he leaped out of the canoe and was gone. When he reached the path to our camper, he turned and faced me. "I'm going bird-watching!" he yelled. "Alone!"

CHAPTER

J UST LIKE THAT, THE CANOE BECAME THE LONELIEST place in the whole world. I sat there for ages, staring at the spot where Jesse had disappeared. Finally, I stepped out into the water, dragged the canoe up onto the shore, and plopped myself down on a big white rock.

Rats!

A movement across the lake caught my eye. Mountain Man was rebuilding his tent, sorting out the poles and tarp and tying things together. I couldn't help wondering — had he been asleep while we were in there? Awake? How much had he heard? Did he know we had opened his briefcase? Had he heard me call him a . . . an ugly old ratbag of a weasel?

I slumped down against the rock. Maybe Jesse was right. Maybe we weren't cut out to be detectives. Maybe all we were good for was —

"Hiya, Stevie!"

Baby-sitting!

"Hi, Alexander."

"I been waiting and waiting for you guys to

come back. Where'd you go? How come you took so long? Did you have fun? Where's Jesse?"

"Gone bird-watching," I said mopily. "Alone."

"I know a place where you can see an eagle's nest," said Alexander. "My mom says it must be big enough for a person to sit in. Wanna see it?"

Why not? Maybe if I could tell Jesse about the world's biggest eagle's nest, he'd start talking to me again.

"Okay," I said. "Show me."

I followed him across the clearing and down a little path past some tents and campers. After a while, I spotted a toilet — an old wooden out-house put up years ago. That reminded me . . .

"Hold on, Alexander. I need to stop in here." There was a piece of wood on a big nail outside to keep the door from swinging open. I twisted it upright, opened the door and stepped inside. I could hear a voice — it sounded like a woman's voice — calling off in the distance.

"You wait out here!" I told Alexander. I didn't want him peeking at me again. Just in case he decided to try it, I locked the door from the inside.

"I get it," he called through the door. "You want privacy, right?"

"That's right. I want privacy." Good! Finally he'd figured it out.

"Here! I'll make it nice and private for you, Stevie." I heard the sound of scraping wood.

"What?" I reached for the door. "Alexander! What are you doing?"

"Stevie, that's my mommy — she's yelling for me. I gotta go! See you later, okay?"

"Alexander! Wait a minute! Don't go!" Quickly, I fumbled with the inside lock to unfasten it. I shoved my shoulder against the door.

Whomp! It didn't move. It didn't even wiggle. I tried again. *Whomp!* Nothing.

"ALEXANDER!!!"

Wonderful! Terrific! Fabulous! The perfect end to a rotten morning! Alexander Creely had locked me in the toilet!

"Help! Let me out! Alexander! Jesse! Dad! Anybody!" I'd been yelling now for at least twenty minutes.

I gave the door a kick. Then another. And another.

Finally, I slumped down on the toilet seat. This was terrible. Horrible. Tragic. I could be stuck in here for hours. Days! Well, maybe not days. Surely someone would come along eventually. Surely my dad would notice I wasn't at dinner and come looking for me.

Half an hour later, I had learned one thing — there is no more boring place in the entire universe than an outdoor toilet. No books, no music — not even a magazine or newspaper.

To pass the time, I started thinking about the case. Mountain Man, for instance — how come he looked so weird? Could his clothes and hair be a disguise? The newspaper article had said that Rubberface Ragnall was a master at changing his appearance. But why would he pick such a scary-looking disguise?

Unless . . . there'd be no better way to avoid snoopy people than to disguise yourself as a crazy old wild man of the woods. After all, it had *almost* worked with Jesse and me.

And what would a mountain hermit want with a briefcase full of Chinese books and papers? Maybe they were secret documents. Or the code to some whole new technology. Maybe they'd been smuggled out of —

Voices! Two of them — coming my way. They sounded angry. My mouth was open, all ready to yell, when I recognized the deeper voice.

"Stay out of it, Max! This is none of your business." It was Jake.

"I'm making it my business," said Max. It was strange to hear him sound so angry. "What are you doing here? *You're* no tree planter!"

Jake snorted. "Let's just say I'm on a little vacation from my real work."

"Well, I don't like it," said Max. "I think it's time Mike Diamond found out who you *really* are."

Jake's answer was clear even though it was almost a whisper. The two of them must have been right outside the outhouse. "I wouldn't do that if I were you, Max. I've got a few things I could tell Diamond about you, too. Things you don't want him to know."

"I . . . I . . ." stammered Max. There was a long silence. I held my breath.

"Exactly!" Jake said softly. "Now why don't we *both* just mind our own business and keep our mouths shut? I promise you, I won't be here any longer than necessary."

Max said something else, but I couldn't make it out. They had already moved on.

I waited a minute, then let out my breath with a big whoosh. If Jake wasn't really a tree planter, who was he? What was he doing here? And what did he know about Max?

My head was spinning. If only I had a partner to talk to. If only Jesse hadn't quit. This case was getting way too complicated, way too confusing. There was no way I could possibly handle it alone.

"Steee-veeeeeee!"

"Here!" I yelled, jumping up. "Over here, Jesse!"

I kept yelling till I heard his voice just outside. "STEE-VEE! Where *are* you?"

"In here! Let me out!"

The door opened a crack. Sunlight poured in. I limped out slowly, like a prisoner released from jail.

Jesse gawked. "What were you doing in *there,* Stevie?"

"You're not going to believe this, but I was detecting."

"Detecting? In there?" He laughed. So did I.

"So, uh, how was bird-watching?"

"Oh," he said, "I didn't go. I didn't feel like it."

"Oh."

Silence.

"So how was detecting?" asked Jesse.

"Not bad. In fact, pretty good."

Silence again. Then we both started talking at the same time.

"Listen —"

"I'm sorry —"

"It was my —"

"No, it was —"

Another weird silence. We both laughed.

"Jesse?"

"Yeah?"

"Do you feel like being partners again?"

He grinned.

"Okay," I said eagerly. "Just *wait* till you hear what I found out!"

CHAPTER

8

I PULLED JESSE ALONG THE PATH TO AN OPEN SPOT
where we hunkered down among some tall
ferns. After looking around to make sure we
were alone, I quickly reported, as exactly as I
could remember it, the conversation between Jake
and Max.

"Good work, Stevie!" Jesse held up a hand and
counted my discoveries on his fingers. "One, Jake
isn't really Jake. Two, he isn't really a tree planter.
And, three, he practically admitted he has a nasty
reason to be here. What do you think? Is it time to
tell your dad?"

I hesitated. "Not yet. The problem is, if we tell
my dad, the first thing he'll do is question Jake
and Max."

"I see what you mean." Jesse chewed on a
fingernail while he thought about it. "Jake warned
Max to keep his mouth shut. Maybe neither of
them would tell your dad a thing."

"Right. Before we go to my dad, we need to
find out more about Jake."

"Do you think Max would tell *us* anything?"

"Hard to say. I guess it can't hurt to ask a few probing questions. We could ask him about himself at the same time. What's *his* big secret?"

Jesse didn't answer. He was staring off into space. After a minute, I gave him a little poke in the rib cage.

"Oh." He blinked. "I was just thinking."

"About what?"

Jesse scratched his head. "Well, all these months we've been trying to find a crime — and nothing. Now, all of a sudden, every step we take — another mystery. Don't you think it's kind of strange?"

"Nope." I jumped up and brushed myself off. "You should read more mystery books, Jesse. Things like this happen to Nancy Drew and Hercule Poirot all the time."

We headed down the path towards the cook tent. Suddenly Jesse stopped. "There's one thing I still can't figure out."

"What's that?"

"The outhouse. It was such a great spot to spy from. How'd you ever think of hiding in there, Stevie? And how'd you lock yourself in?"

I stared at him. Was he serious?

Yes, he was. I sighed and told him the whole story. Funny, I'd been furious at Alexander at the time, but as I told Jesse what happened, I realized that Alexander had really done me a big favour. The outhouse *did* turn out to be a great spying spot.

Not that Alexander *meant* to help me. But he didn't mean to lock me in, either. He never *meant* to do anything. He just did stuff.

Back at the cook tent, you could tell this was a day off. Planters were sitting around in the sunshine, playing board games, writing letters, reading. Jake wasn't there, but Max was sitting on a log with his long legs crossed, reading a newspaper and eating a sandwich. The sight of that sandwich made me remember how long it had been since breakfast.

"See what you can find out from Max," I whispered to Jesse. "I'll get us some food and be right back."

The cook tent was empty except for Rebecca, who was peeling apples. Four pie crusts were lined up in front of her. It didn't take much detective work to figure out she was making apple pies for dinner.

"Hi, Stevie. Lunch is do-it-yourself. There's stuff on the table."

"Thanks."

"Where have you been this morning? Baby-sitting Alex?"

Baby-sitting? Right! Trapped on a toilet seat, yelling my brains out, while Alexander ran free through the woods. "I guess you could call it that," I said.

The lunch table was spread with bread, cheese, cold meats, peanut butter and salmon spread, along with sliced tomatoes, lettuce and fruit. Quickly, I put together four peanut-butter-and-banana sandwiches. Then I noticed the chocolate syrup. "A delicious topping," said the label, "for ice cream and other desserts." Didn't say anything about sandwiches, but that just shows how uncreative the chocolate-syrup people are. I opened up the sandwiches and added a thick gooey layer to each of them. There! Perfect!

Rebecca called as I ran out, "Come back later. I'll sneak you a hot piece of pie."

I expected, of course, to find Jesse hard at work questioning Max. But no, *there* he was — playing some kind of dumb portable video game with Wilbur. When he spotted me, he yelled, "Stevie, you have to see this! Wilbur's got a Ralph the Robot Rat game."

Just what we needed. More Ralph!

Handing him two sandwiches, I glanced at the game over his shoulder. Killer Cats bounced across the screen, making this *sproing, sproing* noise. It looked as if you got five hundred points every time you wiped one of them out. Wilbur's head was bent over the screen as eagerly as Jesse's. Honestly! Jesse and Alexander were bad enough. Wilbur was all grown up. You'd think he'd be way too old for Ralph.

"Jesse," I said, "there's somebody we have to *talk* to, remember?"

"Okay, okay. Just a minute. As soon as I finish this game."

I shrugged and wandered over to Max. When he saw me coming, he folded up his newspaper. "Stevie Diamond! Just the girl I was looking for. How'd you like to play a game of Scrabble?"

"Sure," I said, but I wondered. Could I play Scrabble and detect at the same time? We set the game up across a low stump. Max looked his letters over and then made his first word: CAREFUL.

I stared at it. Was this a message? To me? To himself, maybe? I took a look at my own letters and made *my* first word: CATCH.

As I wrote down the scores, I was thinking hard. How was I going to ask him about Jake in some totally innocent way?

"You sure are a good tree planter," I said.

"Thanks," said Max cheerfully. So far, so good.

"Those greeners aren't nearly as fast as you. I wonder why some of them even come here."

He shrugged.

I took a deep breath. "Like Jake, for instance."

Max glanced up sharply. Uh-oh.

"I don't know anything about that guy," he snapped.

"Okay, fine." I turned quickly back to the board. "Your turn."

Max's next word was FAKE. I stared at it for a minute. Then I formed my next word.

"LIAR," Max read aloud. Slowly, he raised his head to stare at me. All of a sudden, I got very interested in this huge crow cawing in a nearby tree.

The crow flew away. I glanced back at the board to see the word Max had made. HIDE. Hmmmmm . . . A minute later, I made SECRET.

I tried again. "I was just asking, you see, because Jake seems like the kind of guy who —"

Bang! Max's knee jerked up and smacked into the board, knocking it to the ground. Wooden letters flew everywhere. Boy, he really *was* touchy about Jake.

"Listen, Stevie, I guess I'm not really in the

mood for Scrabble after all. I have a headache. I, uh, need to lie down."

He looked awful. His skin had gone all white, so that his freckles stood out like polka dots. Without another word, he stalked away.

I threw the Scrabble pieces into the box and ran over to Jesse, who was still zapping Killer Cats. "I have to talk to you."

"Okay, Stevie, just a minute. I'm already at the third level. I've got four thousand points. Just let me finish this game."

I waited — it seemed to take forever — while Killer Cats bounced stupidly across the screen. *Sproing! Sproing! Zap! Sproing!*

"Seven thousand points!" yelled Wilbur as the game finally finished. "Good going, Jesse!"

"Snick, snick —" said Jesse, and Wilbur joined in. "Booga, booga, snick, snick!"

"Jesse, come *on* — please? We have to talk!"

But it was too late. Who should come rushing up but Milly, dragging Alexander by the hand? He was holding an orange-and-yellow plastic fishing rod with Captain Tuna written across the handle.

"Stevie! Jesse!" Milly sounded desperate. "Could you help me out, please? I need to make pizza dough for dinner, and I can't get anywhere with Alexander underfoot. Can you take him fishing?"

Rats! So much for detecting! Except . . .

"Pizza?" I repeated slowly. "We'd be glad to take Alexander fishing, Milly. And maybe, as a special favour, you could make my favourite pizza."

"Sure." She looked flustered. "Anything. What kind do you like?"

"Anchovies," I said, "and olives."

"Hey!" said Alexander, his eyebrows knit together. "Isn't that —"

"Dee-licious!" I interrupted, rubbing my stomach. "Mmmm. Makes my mouth water." I hammed it up some more until Alexander started giggling.

Jesse stared as if I'd lost all my marbles. As we walked away, he whispered, "Are you crazy? You *hate* anchovies. Everybody in the whole world hates anchovies."

"Everybody," I said, "except —"

Jesse stopped in mid-step and snapped his fingers. "Rubberface Ragnall!" he whispered.

"Exactly! There'll be three or four choices of pizza for dinner tonight. There always are. If Jake takes anchovy-and-olive —"

"We've got him!" said Jesse.

"Well, not exactly. But we're getting closer every second. We're almost there, Jesse. I can feel it in my bones."

"Feel your bones?" chirped Alexander. "I can feel my bones, too. Look! Here's a bunch sticking up right here." He held out his fist with his knuckles showing white. "Feel my bones, Stevie!"

I ran my fingers over his knuckles absent-mindedly. "Great, Alexander. You've got terrific bones." I'd forgotten he was even there.

While Jesse went up to the camper to get some fishing rods, Alexander and I walked down to the lake. On the way, he showed me his knee bones and his toe bones and all the little bones in his spine. By the time we reached the water, I had had it.

"Enough bones!" I said firmly.

"Okay, Stevie." He shut right up. I stared, surprised. Was it possible? Was I finally starting to get the hang of baby-sitting?

Jesse showed up with the rods and we got down to some serious fishing. More or less — I mean, Jesse and I couldn't help talking about the case, and of course, I had to tell him about my weird Scrabble game with Max. Alexander was so excited about fishing that he didn't pay much attention.

Everything went fine until Alexander caught a fish — a small rainbow trout. We could see it flopping around on the surface of the water.

I guess Jesse had never really figured out fishing until that moment. That is, it *sounded* like a good idea to him, and he seemed to enjoy standing there holding the rod. But I guess he never really pictured a dead fish. Problem is, when you go fishing, that's what you're supposed to end up with, right? A dead fish. He turned yellowy green as Alexander hauled it out of the water.

"Throw it back!" he yelled.

"No!" said Alexander.

"No!" I said.

As the fish jerked around on the grass bank, Jesse leaped up, glaring at us. "I refuse to participate in this . . . this slaughter." Without another word, he stomped off.

Sometimes vegetarians can get quite emotional. I have noticed this before.

That left Alexander and me, which *should* have been a total disaster. But Alexander was really interested in learning about fishing, and since my dad had taught me a whole lot, I spent the afternoon showing him techniques and lures and stuff. It felt strange — and I wasn't sure if I liked it or not — to have this little kid looking up at me and waiting for the next word to drop out of my mouth, like it was a jewel or something.

We caught three more fish between us. We even had a few laughs together. Me and Alexander. Weird, eh?

CHAPTER

9

THE PIZZA TRAYS WERE SET OUT IN A ROW. EACH one had a little paper sign on a toothpick sticking out of it. Vegetarian. Mushroom and Pepperoni. Ham and Pineapple. Anchovy and Olive.

Jesse and I stood at the very end of the counter, pretending to talk. What we were *really* doing, of course, was watching the pizza. So far, nobody had touched the anchovy-and-olive. Jesse was right. Nobody in the whole world liked anchovy and olive. Except . . .

There he was. Jake! He was studying the pizzas. Walking back and forth in front of the trays. I felt a little quiver in my knees. He stopped. He picked up a piece of ham-and-pineapple. Rats! He took two steps sideways and took —

Three pieces of anchovy-and-olive!

My heart jumped right into my throat. Beside me, Jesse made a little "eep" sound. We both stared at our feet as Jake passed.

"Did you see that?" gasped Jesse. "Did you —"

"Hey, Stevie!" Rebecca interrupted from the other side of the counter. "Milly said to tell you those pieces on the end are for you. They have extra anchovies and olives. Here, I'll get them for you." She slid three pieces onto a plate and handed it to me.

I stared. The pizza was crawling — absolutely crawling — with squiggly bits of rotten-looking fish and slimy nubs of black olive. "Gee, thanks, Rebecca." I took the plate from her. What *else* could I do?

"Isn't olive-and-anchovy kind of an odd taste for a kid?" she asked. "I figured you for a ham-and-pineapple person."

"Oh no," I said quickly. "It's been my favourite ever since I was, uh — "

"Two!" said Jesse.

"Five!" I said.

Rebecca stared.

"Well, I *started* liking it when I was two, but it wasn't till I was five that it became my absolute favourite." I smiled and took a huge bite. It tasted like something that's been lying around in the back of your locker for about six months.

Rebecca shook her head and wandered off. Jesse, meanwhile, was helping himself to the vegetarian pizza. Glancing over at *my* plate, he snickered. I glared.

"Sorry," he said, sucking in his cheeks.

The only chairs left were right beside Jake! We sat down and I started eating my slimy, rotten pizza. Then I looked around the table.

If someone had asked me to name the most awful bunch of people in the world to eat dinner with, this gang would definitely have been it. There was Jake, of course, right beside me, gobbling down his anchovy-and-olive pizza. Across from him sat Max, still looking pale and jumpy. He glanced nervously at Jake every now and then, but Jake didn't even seem to notice. Lucille looked as grouchy as ever. Her pale blue eyes flitted around the group and stopped when they got to me. It was like looking at a couple of marbles. Right beside her was Wilbur, just taking a seat, his cigarette smoke stinking up the whole table. Way down at the far end of the table was . . . Mountain Man.

Perfect! Just perfect.

Nobody was saying *anything*. It was as if there was a big cloud of black feelings hanging over the table. What a way to eat a meal — just chew, swallow, glare, chew, swallow, glare.

"Hiya, Stevie! Hiya, Jesse! Move over, there's no room for *me*. I got a piece of pineapple pizza and a piece of pepperoni and — yuck, Stevie! — are you going to *eat* that?"

It was actually a relief to hear Alexander's chatter. Not that I really listened to what he was saying. I'd gotten used to tuning him out. Then Jesse nudged me — hard — in the ribs.

"Me and Stevie and Jesse," Alexander was telling Max, "we're all spies! And defectives, too! And you know who we're gonna catch? Jake, that's who. Because he's not even a tree planter, and his name's not even Jake, and that's because he's a crook. Stevie even said so. She said —"

I was on my feet behind him — one arm around his waist and the other hand clamped firmly over his mouth.

"He's, uh, just kidding," I said. I tried to laugh, but it sounded more like I'd swallowed something the wrong way. No one laughed back, except Jesse, who made this really fake heh-heh-heh sound. Jake turned as pale as Max. He didn't move or say a word. Max's mouth dropped open into a big round O. At the end of the table, Mountain Man slowly turned and stared.

"Alexander's just p-playing," I stammered, as I dragged him away from the table. "Boy, what an imagination this kid's got."

Alexander was still squawking as I hauled him out of the cook tent. I was about to yell at him — really let loose — but then I stopped myself. It wasn't his fault. He couldn't help blabbing about every single thing that came into his head. It was *my* fault — mine and Jesse's, for blabbing away in front of him.

"What are we going to *do?*" moaned Jesse.

"I don't know, but whatever it is, we're not going to talk about it till *later* — when we're alone."

"Talk about what?" said Alexander.

For the rest of the evening, the three of us skulked around camp, trying to stay out of the way of Jake and Mountain Man. We told Alexander we were playing hide-and-seek with the tree planters, which was sort of the truth. After we dropped him off at his trailer, Jesse was all for telling my dad the whole story — everything we'd found out so far. But I knew my dad.

"All we have is a bunch of suspicions," I said.

"What about the pizza?"

"Pizza isn't proof. It's not a *crime* to like

anchovy-and-olive pizza."

"It should be," said Jesse, wrinkling his nose. "Anyhow, Stevie, we could be in real danger. Jake knows we're on to him."

"What can he do? My dad and thirty-six tree-planters are here in camp with us. Jake wouldn't dare try anything tonight. And tomorrow, he'll have to go tree planting with all the others."

After arguing some more, we finally compromised. We agreed to give our investigation one more day.

"And if we don't have more evidence by tomorrow night," said Jesse, "we tell your dad. Right?"

"Right," I said, but I wasn't happy. Only one more day to crack the case. Was it possible? And were we really as safe as I had told Jesse we were? The darker it got, the less sure I felt.

For the first time since I'd arrived in camp, I had a hard time falling asleep. Every time a leaf fell or a squirrel twitched, my imagination went wild. What was that? And that?

"Oh, for crying out loud, Stevie," I told myself. "Cut it out!"

So then I did what I always do when I have trouble sleeping. I practised my times tables — starting with one times one and going all the way up to twelve times twelve, except I never get as far as the twelves, which is probably why I don't know them very well.

It worked like a charm. By three times seven, I was snoring.

CHAPTER 10

THE CAMPER WAS SO GREY AND GLOOMY WHEN I woke up that I figured it must be really early. I checked my watch — eight-thirty — and peered out the loft window. The sky was full of thick black clouds, rolling along so fast and low it looked as if they could be ripped open by the tops of the trees. Gusts of wind blew leaves and dirt into tiny whirlwinds. Spruce trees creaked, leaning against each other like a bunch of tired old men.

"Stevie? Are you awake?" Jesse's voice was a whisper behind my curtain.

"Be right with you."

The wind pushed against our thin jackets as we ran down the path. I couldn't wait to get into the cook tent, where there'd be action and people.

Wrong. The cook tent was as dark as a cave and as quiet as a graveyard. Nobody there except Rebecca, who was standing beside the stove, reading a piece of paper.

"A note from Milly," she explained, stuffing it

into her pocket. "She doesn't think I can do anything on my own. Writes instructions for every little thing."

"Where *is* Milly?" I asked, looking around. "And Alexander?"

"Gone to Revelstoke. Milly's doing a food shop today. She took Alexander with her."

"Revelstoke?" Jesse's voice had a choked sort of sound to it. "You mean, you and me and Stevie are *alone* here today?"

Rebecca laughed. The tinkly sound echoed through the tent. "What's the matter, Jesse? Afraid of bears?"

Ouch! I had to practically *lead* Jesse over to a table and sit him down. "I'll get breakfast," I told him.

The pancakes in the oven were rubbery from sitting around for two hours, but I poured syrup on top and took them back to Jesse.

"I don't like it, Stevie," he whispered.

"Me neither," I said, "but it's the only thing left from breakfast."

He shook his head. "Not the pancakes! The *camp!* It's giving me the willies."

He was right. There was something very creepy about the place. The blackness of the sky . . . the howling of the wind . . . the silence in the tent.

"Rebecca?" I said. "When are Milly and Alexander coming back?"

She was stirring a huge pot of steamy stuff that smelled like tomatoes. She looked half hypnotized.

"Rebecca?"

"Huh? Oh, sorry, Stevie. My mind's somewhere

else." She blushed. "It's my boyfriend. I . . . well, I miss him a lot."

Normally, I would have been interested in Rebecca's boyfriend. After all, I'm practically a teenager now, and you never know when I might get a boyfriend myself. At that moment, though, romance was the last thing on my mind. I was thinking about being alone in camp, with only Rebecca for protection. Rebecca — the shortest, skinniest, weakest adult in the whole camp!

The tent grew silent again. It was so quiet and gloomy that I actually started *missing* Alexander. I would have been grateful for some of his noise and jumping around — even one of those boa-constrictor hugs of his. At least he was lively. And — as far as I could tell — he wasn't scared of anything.

"It's going to be a long day," Rebecca said finally. "Not much for you guys to do in this weather. Want something to read? A good murder mystery, maybe?"

"NO!" I said — so loud that Jesse jumped.

"Well, how about some fresh-baked coconut cookies?"

"No thanks," said Jesse.

"No thanks," I echoed.

This was bad. We were even turning down treats. It took a bit of effort, but I finally managed to persuade Jesse to come over to Jake's camper with me.

It was locked up tight. I walked around it twice, trying the doors. "Weird. Tree planters never lock their campers. What's he hiding in there?"

"I don't know and I don't care." Jesse's eyes were darting around nervously. "Let's go back to the cook tent, Stevie. It's creepy out here. This looks like the perfect kind of day for *them* to be out wandering around."

"Them? Them who?"

"You know who," he said grumpily. "Bears!"

There was no point arguing. Jesse was never going to get over his bear phobia. Besides, I wasn't too happy to be roaming around outside today myself. The wind was still fierce and noisy, and the sky was darker than ever.

"Okay," I said. "We'll go back to the cook tent and wait."

"Wait?" he said. "Wait for what?"

"Nothing," I said. But the feeling that something was going to happen got stronger every minute.

Back in the cook tent, I found a deck of cards and started to deal. We were in the middle of a game of snap when Rebecca took off her apron. "I'm going for a nap," she said.

"What?" Jesse jerked around to face her. "You're leaving us? All by ourselves?"

"I've been working since four-thirty this morning, Jesse. I'm dead on my feet." She gave us a puzzled look. "What's gotten into you two? I've never seen you so jumpy."

After she left, the cook tent settled back into a grey silence.

"I wish she hadn't said that," said Jesse.

"What?"

"Dead."

I knew what he meant. The tent suddenly

seemed huge — its corners shadowy and empty, its roof crackling in the wind. The wooden door rattled on its hinges. Jesse looked as if he was holding his breath.

"Your turn," I told him, pointing at the cards. Just at that moment, there was a soft *rat-tat-tat* against the plastic tarp on the roof. We looked up. Raindrops. Just a few. Then more of them, hitting the roof in scattered little bursts. *Rat-tat-tat*, then a pause, *rat-tat-tat, rat-tat-tat*. The sudden rattles of sound made the tent feel lonelier and spookier than ever.

I don't know how much time went by — half an hour, an hour, maybe more — when we heard the motor. Jesse and I stared.

"Must be your dad. Or Milly and Alexander." Jesse got up from the table.

"Wait!" I hissed. "Let's see who it is first." We crept over to the door together and peeked through the opening.

"Uh-oh," said Jesse.

Jake. All alone on a quad. He drove it into the clearing, jumped off and headed towards —

The cook tent!

"Quick!" I said.

As we raced through the back door, I glanced over my shoulder. Oh no! The thin wooden door was swinging shut. When it hit the frame it would make a bang loud enough to wake the dead. I leaped backwards just in time to shove my hand in between.

"Eeee-oww!" It's not easy to yell in a whisper, but I did. The door wasn't heavy, but it stung.

"Stevie! Over here!"

Jesse was huddled behind a huge stump. I joined him, and we waited, holding our breath.

Jake was walking around inside. We could hear his voice, muffled by the wind. "Anybody here? Milly?" Silence. Then, more softly, "Stevie? Jesse? Alexander?"

"Eep!" said Jesse.

"Shhhh!"

A few minutes later, we heard the the front door bang. I poked my head around the stump and spotted him crossing the clearing. He was walking fast, but he wasn't heading for his camper. Or ours. Why? Unless . . . yes! Milly's camper was on that path.

"Come on." I grabbed Jesse's arm. "Let's go after him."

"Are you *crazy*? No way I'm going after that guy. I'm going for Rebecca — right now!"

"Do you know which camper is hers?"

A look of panic crossed Jesse's face. "No! Don't you?"

I shook my head. "Maybe Jake's looking for her. Maybe she's in trouble." I didn't really think Jake was after Rebecca, but if Jesse thought so, maybe it would get him moving.

"Let's go," he said.

I grabbed his hand before he could change his mind. Slowly, we crept around the clearing, staying close to the bushes so we could duck in if we had to. Every few seconds, we stopped to listen. When we reached the path Jake had gone down, we stopped again. This was the tricky bit.

The paths in camp were half-overgrown, and you couldn't always see someone coming towards you. What if he came back?

I went first. We crept slowly along the path, past a small red pup tent, then past a big canvas tent. When we got close to the third campsite, I heard noises. Edging up close, I peeked through a clump of willows.

Jake was inside Wilbur's tent. Sounded as if he was throwing things around — the way he had in Milly and Alexander's trailer. But why? Why Wilbur's place?

Before we had a chance to think about it, he charged out, running down the path.

"Come on," I said. "After him."

As we crept farther along the path, I realized that it led all the way around the outside of the campground to Jake's campsite. I glanced at Jesse. We were both getting soaked. I wished we'd had time to put our jackets on before we'd run out of the cook tent. We passed two more tents and then — yes, there it was — Jake's camper! And *he* was inside. We could hear him thumping around. Now what? We waited.

A minute later, he stepped outside.

"Eep!" said Jesse again. The hair stood up on the back of my neck.

Jake was wearing a raincoat. A red raincoat. It was stained and dirty, and it had a big hood.

But that wasn't all. His moustache was gone. Totally disappeared! And his hair — instead of long, curly dark hair, he had short blond hair cut above his ears.

Jesse's voice was hoarse against my ear. "Is *that* enough proof?" I nodded so hard my teeth shook. Rubberface Ragnall!

He was on the move again. We followed as he stopped at more campsites, doing a quick search around each one. What on earth was he looking for? Soon the path joined the one I'd been on the other day. Yes, there it was — the outhouse. Jake ran past it, then stopped so suddenly I almost charged out in front of him.

That's when it happened. The most amazing piece of luck you can imagine. Jake turned around and walked — are you ready? — right into the outhouse!

Perfect!

I didn't even think about it. I just flew out of the bushes and raced to the outhouse. Grabbing the piece of wood on the nail, I twisted as hard as I could. There!

Jake must have heard me running up. He yelled through the door, "Hey! Who's that?" A second later, when he tried the door, it wouldn't open. He yelled, "Hey!" again and thumped on it.

"That nail won't hold him," I muttered to Jesse. "We need something else." He glanced around and then down at his Wilderness tools. Grabbing his Swiss Army knife, he ran to the outhouse, jammed the knife into a crack in the door frame and ran back.

"Think that'll work?"

"Not for long," I said. "Let's get the quad."

"The quad! What for?"

"To block the door. What else?"

"You mean . . ." said Jesse. "But we can't . . . but, Stevie . . . but I —"

He was still stammering when we reached the clearing. I climbed onto the quad. "Get on," I told Jesse, "and help me remember how to start this thing."

"But it's too big! It won't fit down the path."

"We'll *make* it fit. Get on!"

I couldn't exactly remember how to start the quad. It sputtered and stalled a couple of times while Jesse shouted directions that confused me more than ever. My stomach was tight. What if Jake had already forced his way out?

Finally, the motor kicked into a steady hum. As I drove jerkily across the clearing, Jesse held tight on to my waist. The path *was* a little narrow for the quad. Its fat tires churned over the small bushes and rocks that lined each side as Jesse and I rocked wildly back and forth on the seat. Branches and leaves kept slapping our faces. After a lot of thrashing and roaring and crunching, I finally spotted the outhouse through the trees.

Good! The door still held.

"Hey, Stevie, slow down!" Jesse said into my ear. "You're going to knock the outhouse over!"

He was right. I put on the brakes and, like a plane making a perfect landing, planted that quad right in front of the outhouse door.

I grabbed Jesse, and we ran back down the path. "We got him!" I whooped. Jesse was laughing and smacking me on the back. I felt like Superman. I felt like Wonder Woman. I felt like Sherlock Holmes and Nancy Drew and Hercule Poirot in one!

When we reached the clearing, Wilbur was standing beside the cook tent. As soon as he saw us, he waved and rushed up looking worried.

"Are you kids okay? What happened? Where's Jake?"

"Thank goodness you're here," said Jesse. "We can sure use some backup."

"What's going on? You two look as if you've been through a war."

We both started talking at once. First, we had to tell Wilbur about Rubberface Ragnall and what had happened in Milly's house. Then we had to tell him about Jake being a fake name, and about the pizza and the red raincoat and Jake's hair and moustache. It seemed to take forever before we finally got to the part about the outhouse and driving the quad down the path.

"You mean to say," said Wilbur finally, "that Jake is locked in the outhouse with the quad parked in front of it? You two trapped him in the outhouse?"

"Yes!" we yelled, grabbing each other's hands and dancing around in a circle. We were going to be heroes! We were going to be famous! We'd have our names in the paper again. We'd be —

Wait a minute! How come Wilbur was laughing? It was exciting, but it wasn't exactly funny. He was laughing so hard his face was red. Wiping a tear from his eye, he gave a final chuckle. "I have to thank you two," he said. "You don't know what a huge favour you've just done me."

"You?" I said. It made no sense at all. "How have we done *you* a favour?"

Suddenly he looked really serious. It was amazing how fast his expression changed. It was almost like his face was made out of —

Rubber!

"*I'm* Ronald Ragnall," he said quietly. "The guy you just locked in the outhouse is a cop."

CHAPTER

11

"**O**KAY," SAID WILBUR RONALD RUBBERFACE
Ragnall with a nasty little sneer. "Let's get
down to business."

It only took a split second for my brain to get the
idea to run. Problem was, by the time the message
got through to my feet, Wilbur had already grabbed
my wrist. His other hand grabbed Jesse's wrist.

"I've wasted just about enough time in this
dump," he said as Jesse and I struggled to break
loose. Hopeless! Wilbur's face might have been
like rubber, but his fingers were like steel.
"Where's that kid?"

"Kid?" I said. "You mean Alexander?"

"Yeah! Him and his mom — where are they?"

"They're in R-R-Revelstoke," said Jesse.

"Don't give me that. Where are they?"

"It's true!" I said. "They went shopping this
morning. They've been gone all day. Everyone's
gone. Why do you think we were so glad to see
you?" I was hoping Jesse wouldn't mention
Rebecca. There was still a chance that she'd wake
up and help us.

"Okay," said Wilbur, giving my wrist a little jerk. "Then *you* tell me where it is!"

"Where *what* is?"

"Don't play coy with me. You know what I'm talking about."

"No, honestly," I said. "I don't! We don't!" Jesse, meanwhile, was trying to say something — but he was so scared he was stuttering.

"B-b-b-b-b-b-b —" he was saying. What? What was he trying to say? What *could* he say? He didn't know any more than I did.

"What?" said Rubberface. "Spit it out."

"B-b-b-b-b-b-b —" said Jesse again.

"You got a problem?" asked Rubberface.

"B-b-b-behind you," Jesse finally said.

"Right," snarled Rubberface. "That old trick!"

"B-b-b-b-behind you!" Jesse said again, with a little squeal. "It's a b-b-b-b-b-b-b-bear!"

I twisted around to look. At first, I couldn't see anything, but then I spotted it — a movement over at the far side of the clearing. Yes. It was definitely black. Yes. It was certainly furry. Yes. It was sort of round and rolling as it walked. And yes, those were claws.

I cleared my throat. "Excuse me, Mr., uh, Ragnall, but Jesse's right. That is, uh, quite definitely a bear over there."

"Sure," said Rubberface, but he couldn't help glancing over one shoulder. The bear was ambling slowly in our direction. Rubberface let out a very loud and nasty swear word.

"Don't yell," I said quietly. "Don't yell and —"

Too late. Wilbur dropped our wrists and took

off like a madman, yelling and screaming and waving his arms. He headed straight for the supply shed — the only building in the clearing with real walls.

"Don't run," I finished my sentence, for Jesse's sake. "Don't yell and don't run." I glanced behind us. A broken-down truck was parked at the far end of the clearing. I looked back at the bear. It was loping towards the supply shed.

"Walk backwards," I murmured to Jesse. "Towards the truck. Don't run and don't yell."

Hand in hand, we edged slowly backwards across the clearing. Wilbur was inside the supply shed with the door slammed shut behind him. Nice guy — leaving us out here with a bear! The good news was, all his running and shouting had definitely attracted the bear's attention. It didn't even seem to notice Jesse and me as we backed closer and closer to the truck. It just kept heading towards the supply shack. We could see Wilbur peering out a window, his eyes bulging. We could tell by his open mouth that he was still yelling.

Thank goodness the truck wasn't locked. We scooted inside. Jesse was panting so hard he was steaming up the windows.

"See?" he said between breaths. "Didn't I *tell* you there was a bear around here? Didn't I tell you over and over and *over* that there was a bear? But would you listen? Oh no, you wouldn't listen, you thought I was paranoid, you thought I was crazy, you thought —"

"Okay, okay," I said. "You were right, okay? You were right, already."

The bear was standing on its hind legs, pawing at the supply-shack door. That's when I remembered what was in there. Food! All the food the cooks weren't using for that day. Peanut butter, honey, jam, sugar . . . there might even be pies and cakes. The bear was on all fours now, sniffing at the bottom of the door and scraping at the dirt with its claws.

I couldn't help giggling. "Smart move, Rubberface!" I said. "You've just locked yourself inside a bear's idea of a treasure chest."

Then I remembered Jake. I stopped laughing. Definitely *not* funny!

"Do you know what we've done?" I asked. "We've locked a policeman in a toilet, that's what we've done."

"Actually," said Jesse, "it depends how technical you want to get about it. I mean, if you want to get technical, it was actually *you* who locked him in there."

He was right. *I* was the one who locked a policeman in the toilet, and *I* was the one who drove a quad in front of the door. Boy, I really did it, all right.

"What do you think the penalty is for locking a policeman in a toilet?"

Jesse wiped a clear spot in the steamed-up windshield. "There's probably no specific law against toilets. It probably comes under keeping him from doing his duty — or kidnapping him!"

Kidnapping! What a thought! You could get life in prison for kidnapping. "I'm only twelve years old," I moaned. "I could live to be a hundred!"

I pictured myself, grey haired and stooped, in a

jail cell — a cup of lukewarm water in one hand, a piece of mouldy bread in the other. Water dripping down the walls, rats running across my feet, a bare light bulb shining in my eyes.

There was only one thing to do. I opened the door of the truck.

"Stevie!" Jesse yelled. "There's a bear out there!"

"Don't you think I *know* that?"

Fortunately, the bear and the outhouse were in different directions. I moved as quickly as I could *away* from the bear, tiptoeing across the clearing so that I wouldn't make any noise. The bear didn't even glance my way. It was still trying to figure out how to get into the supply shack — grunting, pawing at the door, scratching at the ground.

As soon as I hit the path, I started to run. Minutes later, I reached the outhouse. The quad was still parked squarely in front of it. A muffled thud or two let me know that Jake was still trying to get out.

Boy, oh boy, oh boy, he was going to be *so* mad at me.

Face the music, Stevie, I told myself sternly. You got him into this mess. Now you get him out! I climbed onto the quad and started the motor. Oh no! It was moving forward. *Crunch!* The next thing I knew, the quad was jammed hard against the outhouse, and the little building was leaning backwards. I hit the brake.

"What's going on?" Jake yelled from inside. "Who's out there?"

"It's me! Stevie Diamond! Excuse me, uh, sir, would you by any chance know how to get a quad to go backwards?"

"What!?" I could hear the alarm in his voice. "A quad? What the heck are you doing out there?"

"I'm rescuing you!" I yelled. Plenty of time later, I figured, to explain how he got trapped in there in the first place.

With Jake shouting instructions, I got the quad into reverse and backed it up. It took bit more work to wiggle Jesse's knife out of the door frame. When I finally opened the door, Jake practically flew out.

"Are you okay?" he said. "Where's Wilbur?"

"This way."

As we ran back to the clearing together, I told him about Wilbur and the supply shack and the bear at the door. Jake snorted, but he didn't say anything. Back in the clearing, Jesse was still locked in the truck. The bear was still pawing the door of the supply shack. And Wilbur was still peeking out the window. When he saw Jake, his eyes bugged out.

"First thing we have to do is get rid of the bear," said Jake calmly. I have to admit, it was nice to have a professional on the job. I followed him over to the truck. He hopped inside and pushed down hard on the horn.

BLAAAT!

The bear jerked and twisted around. You could tell it didn't like the noise much. Jake hit the horn again. BLAAAT! The bear loped off towards the edge of the clearing. Then it stopped and stared back at us. BLAAAAAT went the horn again. The bear disappeared into the woods.

Jake jumped out of the truck with Jesse right behind him. As Jake unzipped his raincoat, I could see the holster strapped across his chest.

"It's all over, Ragnall!" he yelled. "Come on out with your hands up."

Rubberface Ragnall stepped slowly out of the supply shack. His hands were above his head and shaking. His skin was as grey as a city sidewalk, and his eyes looked ready to pop right out of his face.

"Is it gone?" he croaked, peering at the spot where the bear had disappeared. Jake quickly snapped a pair of handcuffs around his wrists.

"What's the big deal?" I said, shaking my head. "It was *only* a bear."

Jesse and Rubberface both glared.

Everything happened at once after that. We heard another engine down the road, and my dad pulled in, driving a crew cab. When he saw Wilbur handcuffed and Jake standing there, blond, with a holster strapped across his chest, he looked stunned. Rebecca rushed into the clearing a minute later.

"I heard the horn," she said, rubbing her eyes.

"What's going on?" asked my dad. "Jake? Is that *you*? Wilbur?"

Jake pulled an identification card from his pocket and showed it to my dad. "Detective David Simms. Vancouver Police. This guy — Wilbur — is actually Ronald Ragnall, also known as Rubberface. He's under arrest. Just let me get him secure and call Revelstoke for help. Then I'll explain everything."

He handcuffed Wilbur-Rubberface inside the broken-down truck and went off to radio to

Revelstoke. Jesse and I started to tell my dad and Rebecca what we knew of the story. When Jake came back, he filled in the blanks. He told us that after the police had tried to arrest Rubberface Ragnall at Milly's house in Vancouver, they'd decided to keep an eye on Milly.

"You're not serious," said my dad. "You don't mean to say that you thought *Milly* was part of a smuggling ring?"

"It's not as strange as you think," said Jake. "He's worked with women before — women you'd never imagine would be a part of something like this. I was assigned to come up here and check her out more. I got an incredible shock when I realized that Ragnall was on the crew."

"How'd you know Wilbur?" I asked.

"I didn't," said Jake, "not right away. The first clue I got was the way he acted out on the block. He was so useless as a tree planter — way worse than everybody else. He complained all the time — about the work and the weather and the bugs. And he was terrified of bears. He was a real city guy. Making lousy money, too. It just didn't make sense. I got to thinking, if he's not earning much money and he doesn't like the wilderness, then why *is* he here?"

Rats! Why hadn't I thought of that?

"Anyway," Jake continued, "I figured out a week or so ago who he was."

"A week ago?" said Jesse. "Why did you wait so long to arrest him?"

"I didn't *want* to arrest him. Not until he had led me to the Banana."

"Banana?" Jesse repeated. "What banana?"

"The Banana. It's a brand-new kind of computer. It's what Ragnall smuggled into the country."

"A computer? And they call it a Banana?"

"Yeah," said Jake. "Apple? Banana? Beats me why computer companies keep naming their products after fruits." He shrugged.

"But that doesn't make any sense at all," I said. "How could a computer disappear in Milly's house or camper? Wilbur and . . . and you, I guess, have been searching everywhere. How could you miss a computer?"

"I don't think it's the actual computer," said Jake. "Just the plan for how to build it, the design. The Banana has just been developed in Japan. It has — let's see if I remember — a hyperactive interactive virtual-reality system."

Jesse let out a low whistle. "I'm impressed."

I stared at him. Did he actually for one single second know what Jake was talking about?

"Apparently it will change the entire way we work with computers," Jake continued. "In December of last year, Wilbur broke into the Banana Corporation and stole the plan."

"What was he going to do with it?" I asked. "Was he going to make computers?"

"He didn't have to. He could sell the Banana plan for millions. There are plenty of companies out there who would take a stolen plan and build computers with it."

"It's called piracy," my dad said. "In the old days, pirates stole jewellery and gold. Nowadays, they steal ideas."

"You mean Wilbur is a pirate?" I asked.

"An electronic pirate, stealing other people's inventions and ideas."

Jesse whistled again. "A smuggler *and* a pirate."

"We got a tip," Jake went on, "telling us where Wilbur was in Vancouver. He was about to make his big sale. We moved in right away, figuring we'd get him and the Banana plan at the same time. But he must have found out we were coming. By the time we got to Milly's house, he was gone."

"And the Banana plan?"

Jake shrugged. "Who knows? I'm not even sure what it looks like. Wilbur stole a computer from the Banana Corporation, but he knew customs officials around the world would be watching for it. He'd have a hard time sneaking an actual *computer* into another country. So maybe he wrote the plan for it down on paper — or maybe it's on computer disks. I just don't know. Ever since I figured out who he was, I've been watching his every move, hoping I could nab him and the Banana plan at the same time."

"And now you've only got him," I said quietly. I knew whose fault *that* was.

"Yes," said Jake, staring at me and Jesse. "It seems that while I was trying to do my job, there were also a couple of amateur detectives on Wilbur's trail."

"Sorry," mumbled Jesse.

"Sorry," I mumbled, too.

"Last night, you two — with Alexander's help, of course — blew my cover as a tree planter. From that moment on, I was just waiting for Wilbur to make his move. I thought he might run for it last night, but he waited till today. I stayed close to him as we were planting. When he jumped onto a quad, I was right behind him on another."

"Behind him?" I said. "But you got here first."

Jake shrugged. "Somewhere between the block and here, I lost him. When I got here, I ran all over the campsite looking for him. But I couldn't find him — or anyone else! I ran for my raincoat and my gun, and then I stopped for a second at an outhouse. The next thing I knew, Ragnall had locked me in. He must have been following me around!"

Jesse and I looked at each other.

"It wasn't exactly, uh, Rubberface who locked you in," I said slowly. "It was us." I looked over at Jesse, then took a deep breath. "Well, actually, it was me."

"You? Why?"

"I thought *you* were Rubberface."

Jake groaned. I closed my eyes. Was he going to arrest me now? But the next person who spoke was my dad.

He didn't have to spell it out, but he did. We had almost ruined Jake's hearing. We had blown his cover as a tree planter. We had locked him — a policeman! — in a toilet when he just was about to catch a criminal. We had risked our lives, we had risked Alexander's life, we had risked Jake's life.

There was more, but you get the general idea.

"Don't be too hard on them," said Jake. "Stevie *did* do a very brave thing today when she came back to the outhouse to let me out."

"Thanks," I mumbled. It was nice of Jake to say that, and I was glad that he didn't seem to want to arrest me. Still, letting him out didn't seem all that heroic considering the fact that I'd locked him in there in the first place.

"You said you thought I was Rubberface Ragnall. Why was that?" asked Jake.

I told him the whole story, starting with how we figured out on the block that Jake wasn't his real name — unless he was hard of hearing.

"So *that* was why you smashed that bag behind my head."

I blushed. "Right," I said in a tiny voice.

"Go on," said Jake. So I told him about that time I was locked in the outhouse while he was arguing with Max.

"Oh, that," he said. "Well, I don't like to say too much about it, but I was the arresting officer on a case a few years ago. Max got himself in some trouble — he was just a teenager back then and, well, I guess he wants to forget about it. He wasn't very happy when I showed up in camp — especially in disguise and using a false name."

"Why were you in disguise?" Jesse asked.

"I was worried that Milly would recognize me," Jake said. "I was around her house in Vancouver quite a bit when we were searching it."

He rubbed at his short blond hair. "I guess you kids were watching when I got rid of the wig?"

We nodded.

"And that made you even more certain that I was Rubberface?"

"That and the raincoat and the pizza," I said.

Jake looked confused, so we explained.

He laughed, but it was a sad little laugh. "Half the planters in camp have red raincoats. All the stores in Vancouver are selling them this year. If we'd had a few more rainy days, you would have realized that."

"But what about the pizza?" asked Jesse.

Jake shook his head. "Didn't you two notice what kind of pizza *Wilbur* was eating?"

I gulped. We'd been so sure it was Jake that we had left the counter as soon as he picked up his slices. "Anchovy-and-olive?" I said slowly.

Jake nodded. "Six pieces. Wilbur polished off the whole tray."

12

"STUPID, STUPID, STUPID," I SAID THE NEXT AFTERNOON. "How could we be so stupid?"

Jesse and I were slumped around the table in our camper, feeling about as low as you can possibly feel without digging a hole. I kept seeing Jake's face — the way it had looked when he'd left camp. While we were waiting for the Revelstoke police, he'd tried to question Wilbur. The only thing Wilbur would say was "Get me a lawyer." Pretty soon a squad car arrived and left again with Wilbur and Jake. I couldn't help noticing how quiet Jake was as he got into the car. All that time, all that work — and he still hadn't found the Banana plan.

And whose fault was that? Ours!

"We're idiots!" I said. "They should take away our business cards. They should tear up our detective licences."

"We don't *have* detective licences," Jesse reminded me.

"Then they should make a law," I muttered.

"What kind of law?"

"A law to make sure we never *get* detective licences."

"Oh, Stevie," said Jesse wearily. "We've been talking about this all day. What's the point? It's like my mom always says — there's no use crying over spilled milk."

"Who's crying? Lucille's the one who's crying, not me."

When the planters returned from work and found out what had happened, they were all shocked, but Lucille just let out this little cry — as if someone had hit her — and ran off to her tent without a word. This morning at breakfast, her eyes were all red and puffy, and she kept blowing her nose.

"I think Lucille really liked old Wilbur," said Jesse.

"More than *liked*," I said. "She must have been crazy about him to get that upset."

Jesse nodded. "Poor Lucille. I guess some people wouldn't recognize a crook if he punched them right in the nose."

"Some people? What about us? Wilbur had to *tell* us he was Rubberface Ragnall. Some detectives we are!"

Jesse drummed on the table with his fingertips. Then he started picking at the plasticky covering that was coming loose on the table. I just sat there, staring at a trapped fly that was dive-bombing the window screen. It took a few more angry buzzes at the window before drifting in a slow, lazy circle around the camper. I followed it with my eyes.

Somehow this holiday just wasn't turning out the way I'd planned.

We could hear Alexander's voice from a long way off, but neither of us moved. By the time he ran in the door, he was practically hysterical. "Stevie! Jesse! Everything's all over — everything! My Killer Cats, my train set, my crayons, my blocks, my —"

"Slow down, Alex," said Jesse. "What's the problem?"

"Our camper! It's all messed up again. And I didn't dooooooo it!"

Was this a joke? No, he was quivering. I caught Jesse's eye. Wilbur was in jail in Revelstoke — we'd seen him get into the police car with our very own eyes. He was wearing handcuffs, and there were three huge policemen with him. No way he could have escaped.

"This is crazy!" I shook my head. "Wilbur's miles away!"

"Maybe it wasn't Wilbur."

"Jesse, if you try to tell me it was a bear, I'll —"

"No, no, Stevie, not a bear. Think about it. Do smugglers work alone?"

I slapped my forehead. "Of course. Jesse, don't you remember? When Milly told us about Rubberface in the first place, she said the police suspected her of being part of a smuggling *ring*."

"Ring?" said Alexander. He held up the Ralph the Robot Rat ring on his finger. You could hardly see the rat face under all the jam.

"Not that kind of ring, Alexander. I'm talking about a bunch of smugglers who work together.

Or maybe just two." I stared at Jesse. "Do you really think it's possible? That Wilbur has a *partner* here in camp?"

"It's the only possible explanation. And now Jake's gone. What are we gonna do?"

I knew what we *should* do, of course. Tell my dad. Tell Alexander's mom. Call the police. But I couldn't help thinking — if there *was* still a crook in camp, Jesse and I would get another chance as detectives.

I headed for the door. "Let's go."

"Go? Where?" Jesse and Alexander scrambled to keep up with me. The fly, seeing his chance, made a daring escape at the same time.

"Wilbur's tent. Maybe we can find something that will lead us to his partner."

"But we already *know* who his partner is," said Jesse. "Lucille! She was crying about him."

"You could be right," I said. "But this time, we're going to be sure!"

The police had done a search through Wilbur's tent, but it didn't look as if they'd taken much with them. His stuff was still there, sort of messed up and thrown around.

"You start at that end," I told Jesse, "and I'll look over here."

"What about me?" asked Alexander.

"You look in the middle." The middle had nothing but clothes in it. I figured he couldn't do much harm there.

My end had Wilbur's suitcase. It was open, and it was obvious that the police had already gone through it. There were clothes and some shaving and washing stuff. A carton of cigarettes, too, and some matches. Only one book — *Jaws of the Grizzly: Famous Bear Encounters*. No wonder Wilbur was so scared in the supply shack. I threw the book down. I was looking for an address book or a diary, but it was probably hopeless. If the police had found something like that, they would have taken it with them.

"Find anything, Jesse?" I said. Alexander was playing dress-up with Wilbur's clothes.

"Nothing much. Looks like Wilbur might have been writing something, but whatever it was, it's gone now." He held out a pad of paper. The top sheet was blank, but you could see the dents on it where a pencil or pen had pressed through from another sheet on top.

"Wait a minute!" I said, getting excited. "Let me see that, Jesse!"

"What for?"

I spotted a pencil in the corner and grabbed it. Laying the note pad flat on the floor, I started rubbing the pencil lead lightly over the top sheet of paper.

"What are you doing?" asked Jesse.

"I'm trying to make the outlines of the letters show up," I said. "Detectives do it in books all the time. Sometimes you can see all the writing on the page this way."

"Well, it's not working this time," Jesse mumbled, peering over my shoulder.

"Not perfectly," I agreed, rubbing more. "But see? There are little bits showing up here and there."

Outside in the sunlight, we could make out a few scattered words and letters.

"Look," said Jesse. "There's 'Jake' and 'cop.' And look here — it says 'ave to leave.' That must be 'have to leave.'"

"It's a letter," I said. "It's a letter to his partner. Jesse, this is it! He must have written a note to his partner the night before he got caught."

"Keep looking, Stevie. What else can you read?"

I stuck my face close to the paper and searched it line by line. "Not much. Just a few words. Here — it says 'last try' and what's this? 'Ship'? No. 'Chip.' And here's 'kid.' And there's all this stuff in between. You try!"

Jesse squinted at the paper. "It's a letter, all right. Look at the signature."

It wasn't very clear, but if you looked closely and knew what you were searching for, you could see it. "Ronald."

"What's that word just above it?" I said. "It's something and then 'a-t-c-h'?"

"Match?" said Jesse. "Catch? Patch?"

"Look at me!" Alexander interrupted. "I'm a defective!"

"Defective?" I glanced up. "Oh, you mean detective. Nice costume, Alexander."

He was wearing a lime green cap that said I Love Detroit. Most of his body was covered by a huge pair of shorts with orange walruses all over them. That Wilbur — he must have been some classy dresser! Alexander had pulled the shorts up so high that the waistband was right under his armpits. A clothespin at the front held them up. The bottoms of the shorts stopped just above his ankles, so we could see his bright red socks and the Ralph the Robot Rat watch. On his feet were a pair of huge black-and-white striped sneakers.

I looked at Alexander. Then I looked at the letter. I looked back at Alexander. Then I looked at the letter again. Then I looked at Alexander one more time.

Oh my gosh! Oh my gosh oh my gosh oh my gosh.

"Stevie!" said Jesse. "What are you doing? What's wrong?"

I tried to speak, but only a whisper came out.

"Stevie, what's wrong? Have you got something caught in your throat?"

He had to hit me on the back twice before I could speak. "Jesse," I croaked finally. "I've got it!"

"Got what? A disease?"

"No! I've got *it!* All of it! I've figured it out! Go to the radio phone and call the police in Revelstoke. Tell Jake to get right back here as fast as he can."

"You mean you know who Wilbur's partner is?"

I nodded.

"Who, Stevie? How do you know?"

"There's no time to explain. Go! Now! Get Jake on the radio phone. He's taking Wilbur into Vancouver today. He might have already left."

"Why can't *you* call him?"

"Because I have to think."

"Think about what?"

"What I'm going to do," I said. "Go!"

"What am I supposed to say?"

"Tell Jake to get in his car right this instant. Tell him — tell him I have the Banana plan."

"Stevie! You don't!"

"Of course not. But I know where to get it . . . I think."

"Oooooh boy." Jesse shook his head and let out a deep sigh. "I sure hope you know what you're doing. Do you have any idea how much trouble we're going to be in if you turn out to be wrong?"

I knew. It was a hundred-kilometre drive from Revelstoke. Jake was probably really tired. And he was already mad at me. If I was wrong . . .

"I'm not wrong." I crossed all my fingers and my thumbs, too. "Go! Call him! Now!"

I stood there watching as Jesse ran off.

"Wait for me!" yelled Alexander, hauling on his pants.

I glanced again at the faint lines on the paper. I wasn't wrong. I *couldn't* be.

Could I?

CHAPTER

13

THE COOK TENT WAS SLOWLY FILLING AS THE planters drifted in from work. One or two sounded annoyed to hear dinner would be late. Mostly, though, they just looked confused to see Jake and the other policeman back in camp. They took their places around the big tables, mumbling quietly.

I did a final check of the tent. Jake was sitting right up front, close to where I was standing. He tapped his fingers together impatiently. Beside him, a big, bald policeman from Revelstoke spread out over a chair and a half. He and Jake were watching me. They *weren't* smiling. My dad leaned forward in his chair, looking worried. Behind him sat Milly and Alexander and Rebecca in a little cluster. I looked around for Lucille. There she was, her pale eyes still looking a bit red and weepy, her hands twisted together in her lap. A few chairs over, Max was chewing on his lower lip as he stared at the floor. And off by himself as usual — a whole table separating him from everyone else — sat Mountain Man. His dark eyes burned into mine without blinking. I glanced away quickly.

Jesse and I stood at the front, facing everyone. Well, actually, Jesse was sort of behind me, doing his best to be invisible. I couldn't help feeling he wasn't exactly a hundred per cent on my side.

"Is all this really necessary, Stevie?" Jake asked for the third time. "Why don't you just tell me what you know?"

"Really soon," I promised. "Just trust me, okay?"

He glanced at the other policeman, who shrugged and rolled his eyes. "This better be good," said Jake. "I broke all the speeding records in B.C. to get here."

I smiled confidently as if I knew exactly what I was doing. Deep inside, a shudder passed through me. This time, I'd better be right!

"Okay," I said, and then, "Hey, everyone!" My voice came out just a little bit squeaky. I took a deep breath and thought of Hercule Poirot. Clearing my throat, I started again. "Ladies and gentlemen, may I have your attention, please?"

Gradually the voices in the room quietened down. "You all know what happened yesterday," I said a bit shakily, "how the notorious smuggler, Wilbur Rubberface Ragnall, was captured right here in camp." People nodded and grunted. I continued in a stronger voice. "Jesse and I have important information to reveal at this time."

I held up the piece of paper that Jesse and I had found in Wilbur's tent. "If nobody minds, we will call this piece of paper Exhibit One."

Jake leaned forward and squinted. "What is it?"

"A letter," I said. "At least, it's a piece of paper that was lying *underneath* a letter that Wilbur wrote. Jesse and I pencilled over the marks to try to see what it says. We think Wilbur wrote the letter to his partner."

Suddenly the tent was a babble of noise. The word "Partner!" flew around like a Ping-Pong ball.

"Jesse and I have only been able to make out a few of the words," I admitted. "You tell them, Jesse." I turned around and handed him the paper.

He didn't have any choice. He coughed loudly and started to read. "'Jake. Cop. Have to leave. Last try. Chip. Kid. Atch. Ronald.'"

Lucille jerked up out of her seat. "This is ridiculous!" she called out in a shrill voice. Her hands were trembling. "Somebody make them stop this nonsense!"

"Now, now, Lucille." My dad half turned in his chair to face her. "Let's give them a chance. Go on, Stevie."

Clearing my throat again, I continued. "You'll notice that most of the words Jesse mentioned aren't hard to figure out. Wilbur was telling his partner that 'Jake' was a 'cop' and that he, Wilbur, would 'have to leave' camp and was going to make a 'last try' at something."

"Sounds reasonable," said my dad. "But what about 'chip'? And 'atch'?"

"I was just coming to that." I turned to face Jesse. "Jesse, may I remind you of what we do most days in Mr. Dipster's class?"

"You mean brainstorming?"

"Precisely!" Mr. Dipster taught us science. Brainstorming was his favourite activity in the whole world.

"What's brainstorming?" asked Milly.

"It's when you say every idea that comes into your mind as fast as you can," Jesse explained. "You try to come up with as many ideas as possible."

Milly snorted. "Why are we wasting our time —"

"Wait." Jake held up a hand. "I'm intrigued. Let's hear the kids out."

"Here's how it works," I said. "Jesse — the word *chip*. What comes to your mind when you hear the word *chip*?"

"I know!" yelled Alexander. "Fish and chip! I love fish and chip!"

"Fish and *chips*, Alexander," I said. "Very good. Now let Jesse try."

Jesse looked around and gulped. "Potato chip," he said slowly. "Chipped tooth. Chip off the old block."

"Good. Keep going."

"Uh, wood chip. Chip and Dale. Am I getting warm?"

"You're doing great. Keep going."

"Poker chip? Chipmunk?" He paused, and I thought that was it. Suddenly his eyes got huge. His mouth dropped open.

"MICROCHIP!" he yelled.

"A microchip!" said Jake. "Of course! That's how Ragnall smuggled in the design for the Banana computer. On a microchip!"

"What's going on?" asked Alexander. "What's a

microchip?"

"It's like the brains of a computer," Jesse explained. "It's this teeny-weeny little thing that tells the computer what to do."

"How teeny-weeny is it?" asked Milly.

Jesse's face fell. "*Very* teeny-weeny," he said in a gloomy voice. "Do you know how small those suckers are, Stevie? Not much bigger than one of your freckles. We could spend the rest of our lives looking for it."

"Not necessarily," I said. "Let's take a look at the other strange word in Wilbur's letter. *Atch*. It's not even a word because we can't read the first letter. But maybe Jesse and I can *make* it a word by brainstorming."

"Let me see," said Jesse, biting his lip. "Batch. Catch. Uh, hatch." He was doing what I had done, going through the alphabet. "Latch. Match. Patch. Watch."

"Stop right there!" I said.

"Watch?" Jesse's eyes started blinking rapidly. "Wait a minute. The letter said 'kid,' too." Suddenly he stared at me and clapped both hands over his mouth. "Alexander's watch! The microchip for the Banana computer is in Alexander's watch!"

"What watch?" My dad was peering down at Alexander's bare arms. "Alexander doesn't even have a watch."

"Oh yes, he does," said Jesse. "Show them, Alexander."

Alexander grinned and held up his ankle. Ralph the Robot Rat blinked on and off at us.

"Ladies and gentlemen," I said. "Exhibit Two."

"Wilbur had one just like it!" Jesse's voice was shaky with excitement. "He showed it to me when we were playing video games. I bet he had it all ready to switch with Alexander's watch."

"Right!" I said. "Except he could never find Alexander's. And why not? Because it's been on his *ankle* all along, hidden under his jeans."

"Gosh," said my dad. "Do you think there really could be a microchip in that watch, Jake?"

"Easily," said Jake, his voice almost as excited as Jesse's. "In fact, there's probably one to make the watch work. The question is, is there a *second* micro-chip in the watch — one that doesn't belong there? Alexander, where exactly did you get that watch?"

"I . . . uh, found it. I didn't steal it, honest."

"Where, Alexander? Where was it when you found it?"

"Dunnabackacowtch," Alexander muttered into his shirt.

"Could you say it a bit louder?"

"DOWN THE BACK OF THE COUCH!" yelled Alexander. "It was in my secret hiding place, underneath all the cushions on the couch. It was there when Mommy and me came back from Edmonton. The Easter Bunny left it for me."

"Alexander!" Milly groaned. "Why didn't you tell me?"

"I did!" said Alexander. "I *told* you I found it in the couch, and I *told* you the Easter Bunny left it. You said it was my 'magination. I told a policeman, too, when he was searching, but he didn't listen. *Nobody* ever listens to a five-year-old!"

Suddenly I could remember what it was like, being five. Alexander was right.

"Except Stevie and Jesse," said Alexander quickly. "You guys listened to me real good."

"People don't listen all that well to twelve-year-olds, either," I told him.

Milly looked upset. She grabbed Alexander into a big hug. "Sweetie, I'm sorry I didn't listen to you."

"Well, we're all listening now," said Jake. "Alexander found the watch stuffed down the back of the couch. Wilbur must have put it there when he realized the police were outside, figuring he could come back for it later. What he didn't know was that Alexander would find it and start wearing it on his ankle. Alexander, do you mind if I take a look at that watch?"

"Why?" Alexander plopped his backside down on the ankle wearing the watch. "What are you going to do with it?"

"Alexander, I promise — on my word as an officer of the law — to give your watch back to you in exactly the same shape as I get it. Or, if I can't, I'll buy you another."

"Well," said Alexander, slowly edging off his ankle, "well, okay. If you promise." He handed the watch to Jake.

Jake laid it down carefully on a nearby table. My dad found a tool kit, and one of the planters offered some little tools that you use to fix eyeglasses. The tent was so silent we could hear the tiny chink and scrape of metal as Jake worked on the watch. After what seemed like forever, he finally pulled the back off. Carefully, he lifted the watch and turned it upside down.

Tink! A tiny something fell out onto the tablecloth.

"Is that it?" Jesse whispered.

"I believe . . . I think . . . yes, here's the one that makes the watch work, it's still inside . . . yes, yes, yes! This is it!" Jake did a little leap into the air. "YES!" he shouted.

Suddenly the room was a buzz of excited chatter. Jake picked up the chip with his fingertips and put it into a tiny plastic bag that Milly brought from the kitchen.

"Stevie and Jesse," he said. "I don't know how to thank —"

"Wait a minute." I raised my voice again, and the chatter stopped. "We're not done yet. Who did Wilbur write the letter *to*?"

"Yeah," said Jesse. "We still have to find out who Wilbur's partner is."

Jake shrugged. "A letter could go anywhere. Don't you worry, Stevie, the police will —"

"Uh-uh." I shook my head. "It's someone right here in camp." Reaching into a paper bag near my feet, I pulled out a pair of black-and-white striped sneakers and held them up. "Ladies and gentlemen, Exhibit Three!"

"A pair of shoes?" said my dad. "So what?"

"Wilbur's shoes," I said. "Do you notice anything about them?"

My dad shook his head. "Black and white stripes. Nice leathery look to them. Like a zebra maybe?"

"Exactly!" I said. "They come from a shop in Vancouver called Jungle Duds. These sneakers were bought as a gift for Wilbur by his girlfriend who is right here, right now, in this tent — and wearing a pair of tiger-striped sneakers herself!"

Suddenly all I could see was the tops of heads as everyone peered at everyone else's feet. Only one head in the whole crowd *didn't* look down. Her grey eyes stared straight into mine.

CHAPTER

14

S LOWLY, REBECCA ROSE TO HER FEET. EVERY EYE IN the tent turned to where she stood, frozen, in front of her chair. This was it — the moment of truth! Was I right? As the seconds ticked by, it seemed as if time had stopped. We sat there, rigid as statues — me, Jesse, Milly, Jake, my dad, all of us — staring at Rebecca, whose mouth and eyes were giant circles on her face. Her hands were clasped so tightly that I expected to hear bones snap.

Then slowly her mouth started to move. "I . . . " she said, and again, "I —"

Suddenly, she whirled and ran. Almost before I could blink, she was out the door into the night.

"Stop her!" yelled Jake.

There was a noisy scramble full of grunts and shouts and the clatter of folding chairs as everyone headed for the door.

"Hurry!" yelled Jake as three planters tried to push through the door at the same time. "She'll get away."

Seconds later, the tent was silent and half deserted. I dropped into the closest chair with a sigh of relief.

"Stevie, come on!" yelled Jesse, dancing around near the door. "Hurry up! She's going to get away."

"No, she won't. Relax, Jesse. They'll bring her back in just a minute."

He stared. "How do you know?"

"I just do," I said. Alexander giggled, and I gave him a wink.

"I know, too," Alexander said with a laugh. "Me and Stevie, we both know."

Just as I expected, everyone returned to the cook tent within minutes. Jake and the other policeman had Rebecca firmly between them. She was wearing handcuffs and glaring at Jesse and me as if she'd like to mop the floor with us.

"We found the letter in her pocket," Jake said, holding up a folded piece of paper. It looked a lot like the "instructions from Milly" that Rebecca had been reading when Jesse and I came into the cook tent the morning before. "Here, Stevie, you do the honours."

In a slow, clear voice, I read the letter aloud to the group. "'Dear Rebecca, Jake is a cop. He's on to me, and I have to leave tomorrow. I'll go to work in the morning as usual, but I'll sneak back early. Stay out of the way so they don't suspect you. I'm going to make one last try to get the chip. I'm sure the kid knows where it is. If I don't find it, you keep trying. We have to find that watch. Love, Ronald.'"

There was a silence. Then Jake said, "Stevie, you're amazing. How on earth did you figure out that the two of them were partners?"

"Well, I wasn't absolutely sure until ten minutes ago. I remembered that when we first met Rebecca, she showed us her shoes and said she'd bought a zebra-striped pair for her boyfriend. So when I spotted this pair in Wilbur's tent, it looked really suspicious. But I couldn't prove anything — not till Rebecca made a run for it."

"You stinking little rats!" snarled Rebecca. "After all I've done for you! Cookies, pies, special olive-and-anchovy pizzas —"

"Hah!" snapped Jesse, staring her straight in the eye. "It takes more than cookies and pizza to buy off Diamond & Kulniki. Stevie and I are professionals!"

"You sure are." Jake grinned. "I'll make sure you get full credit for this capture."

"Oh, we didn't do it *all*," I said modestly. "You caught Rebecca when she tried to run away."

Jake shrugged. "Pure luck. Rebecca ran straight for her car and was about to drive off. Lucky for us, her car wouldn't start."

Alexander giggled.

"Well, it wasn't exactly luck," I said slowly. "Show them, Alexander."

He held up a small piece of metal.

"What's that?" asked a voice from the back.

"The rotor arm from Rebecca's car," said Alexander proudly. "Me and Stevie got it out. The car can't go without it"

"What?" Jake's mouth dropped open.

I nodded. "I figured that if I was right about Rebecca, she might try to make a getaway. Our, uh, junior junior partner here, Alexander Creely, is a car expert. I asked him if there was something we could do to her car so it wouldn't work — temporarily, of course."

"It was easy," said Alexander. "But you told me it was a joke, Stevie. You said it was a spy-club joke."

"Alexander, if I'd told you the truth, everyone in camp would know. Right?"

"Right," he said, looking embarrassed. "I'm not real good at keeping secrets yet." His lower lip quivered.

My dad ruffled his hair. "Listen, Alex, when Stevie was five years old, *she* wasn't very good at keeping secrets, either."

"Really?" Alexander brightened.

"Really," said my dad. "In fact, you're a *lot* like Stevie — in more ways than you know."

Alexander beamed. He looked as if he'd just won a million dollars.

"Dad?" He and I were walking back to our camper in the dark. The police had left, taking Rebecca with them. We'd finally eaten dinner, and nearly everyone — Jesse included — had packed it in for the night. "What did you mean? About Alexander being a lot like me?"

"Don't *you* think he's a lot like you?"

"No way!" What a thought! "It's not that he's a bad kid or anything. Sometimes I even almost like him. But let's get real, Dad — he's nothing like *me*."

"Okay, Stevie. Try this. How would you describe Alexander?"

"That's easy. He's — what do you call it? — impulsive. I mean, he keeps doing things without thinking. And he's nosy, always poking his nose into everyone's business. Oh, and he can't keep still — not even for a single second — and he's really, *really* messy. And talk? He'll talk your ear off. You've never heard anybody talk the way —"

I stopped. My dad was grinning from ear to ear. There was a long pause.

"Well, okay," I muttered, "but I was never *that* bad."

My dad threw an arm across my shoulder. "Did I ever tell you," he asked, "how much I *like* Alexander?"

"Tell me," I said. We wandered slowly down the path together.

CHAPTER

15

"T HIS IS THE LIFE!" I DROPPED MY FISHING ROD
and stretched my arms high above my
head. "I think I've had just about enough
detecting for one vacation."

Jesse, Alexander and I were sprawled in the
long grass beside Ruby Lake. Alexander and I
both had fishing lines in the water, although I'd
have been just as glad if the fish left my line
alone. After the last couple of days, I didn't feel
like fighting with anything — even a fish. Jesse
had a pair of binoculars glued to his nose and was
scanning the sky for hawks and eagles. Beside us
was a half-full bag of marshmallows that we'd
talked Milly out of.

"Yes, sir," I said. "Fishing, hiking, bird-watching,
rock climbing — that's what we came here for in
the first place. And what have we been doing
instead? Chasing smugglers! Hunting for
microchips!"

"I'm surprised at you, Stevie." Jesse was
scanning the shoreline now. "You were the one
who was so keen on this investigation. You were

the one who couldn't leave it alone for even one hour since we've been here — except when you were asleep. And you were the one who had to figure out every last detail of the crime."

"Yeah, Stevie," said Alexander enthusiastically. "You must be the greatest defective in the whole wide world."

"For the last time, Alexander — it's *detective!*"

"That's what I said. Defective."

I wiggled my bare feet in the grass. "My brain hurts," I said. "Do you know how much thinking it took to figure everything out?"

"Well, give your brain a rest," said Jesse. "Wilbur and Rebecca are all locked up now. That leaves just you, me, Alexander and the Wilderness. I'm warning you, though — if one of you guys catches a fish, I'm out of here!"

"Speaking of Wilderness," I said, "somehow we missed the biggest clue of all."

"What's that?" Jesse asked.

"Wilbur himself! I mean, here was a guy who hated the outdoors, loved video games and smoked cigarettes. He stood out like a sore thumb. How could we miss him?"

Jesse dropped his binoculars and lay back in the grass. "How can you think about Wilbur on a beautiful day like this?"

It *was* a beautiful day. Not a cloud in the sky, not a ripple on the lake. The only sounds were the rustle of wild grass and the rumbling of frogs in the bulrushes. We'd already gone swimming twice today — our first swims all week, if you don't count Jesse's accidental dunk in the lake. It was hard to believe that only yesterday the three of us were madly searching through Wilbur's tent, trying to figure out who his partner was. It seemed like a million years ago.

Across the lake, a thin wisp of smoke rose from the campfire by Mountain Man's tent. He was taking the day off to rest a knee that was giving him trouble.

Jesse noticed where I was looking. "Hey, Stevie, I saw you talking to Mountain Man after dinner last night. How did you two get to be so buddy-buddy?"

"His name is Jeremy Hawthorne," I told him, "and we're not exactly buddies. I guess I was in a brave mood last night. I decided to ask Mountain Man — I mean, Jeremy — about those papers and books in his briefcase. The ones in Chinese."

Jesse's head popped out of the grass. "You did?"

"You're not going to believe this, but he used to be a professor."

"You mean, like at a university?"

"Of course," I said. "Where else do they have professors — at the 7-Eleven? He used to be a professor of Asian Studies. He speaks five languages! Two kinds of Chinese, I forget what they're called, and Japanese, and some other language. Oh, and English."

"You're kidding!" said Jesse.

"I knew that," said Alexander.

"What?" I gawked at him.

"Sure," he said. "Mountain Man told me a whole bunch of stories about when he was in China and Japan — and some other funny-sounding place that sounds like you have to wear a suit there."

"Thailand?" I suggested.

"Yeah. Tie-land. He had a gov-gov-govmint job in a big city there with millions of people. Starts with a bang."

"Bangkok?"

"Yeah, that's it. Bangkok."

I groaned. "Alexander, why didn't you tell us about this?"

He shrugged. "You never asked."

True. We had never asked.

"I wonder why he quit," said Jesse. "Being a professor, I mean. Why would he become a hermit?"

"Probably some terrible tragedy," I said. "Probably he was rejected by the only woman he ever loved, so —"

"Nope," interrupted Alexander.

"Beg your pardon?"

"He just got tired of being a professor, Stevie. He told me it was boring. Said he likes trees and mountains and wild animals way better."

"Oh." Suddenly, I couldn't think of anything else to say.

"So tell me, Alexander," I said after a minute, "do you know absolutely everything?"

"Nope. I don't know how to tie my shoelaces. And I don't know how much is two plus seven neither."

"Nine," said Jesse quickly. "And we'll teach you to tie your shoelaces. But listen, what about Lucille? Can you tell us anything about her?"

"What do you want to know?" Alexander pulled

his line out of the water and stared at it glumly. "Stevie, do you think if I put a marshmallow on my hook, the fish would like it better?"

"Fish don't like marshmallows, Alexander." I turned to Jesse. "I've been wondering about Lucille, too. I mean, I know she really liked Wilbur, and I know he was only pretending to like her so she'd help him with tree planting. What I *don't* know is, why was she acting so suspiciously? What was she doing that night she snuck off into the woods with her flashlight and binoculars?"

"She does that a lot, almost every night," said Alexander.

"She does?"

He nodded. "Owling."

"Owling?"

"Yeah. You know — looking for owls."

"You mean," cried Jesse, "that all this time I've been here in camp with a serious *bird-watcher* and I didn't even *know* it? Alexander, why didn't you —"

Alexander and I answered at the same time. "You didn't ask!"

I lay back in the grass again. "Unbelievable."

For a few minutes, nobody spoke. I was trying to figure out how much time Jesse and I could have saved if only we'd done a better job of quizzing Alexander.

"Stevie?" Alexander sounded timid.

"Yeah?"

"Well, I was wondering. Like, when we all go back to the city? My baby-sitter, Mrs. Wooster? She's not nearly as much fun as you and Jesse, and she's not a member of the Ralph the Robot Rat Spy Club neither, and she watches kissing shows on TV and makes me eat sardine sandwiches for lunch, and I was thinking . . ."

"Yeah?"

He spoke quickly. "Would-you-and-Jesse-be-my-baby-sitters-back-in-Vancouver-I-already-asked-Jesse-and-he-said-yes."

It was obvious he expected *me* to say no. His forehead was wrinkled with worry, and his mouth was kind of scrunched up. As I watched, his glasses slid down to the end of his nose and hung there like a car teetering on the edge of a cliff.

"Alexander," I said slowly, "it would be a" — I paused to search for exactly the right words; he caught his breath — "a thrill and an adventure to be your baby-sitter."

His forehead wrinkled even deeper. "Does that mean yes?"

I nodded.

"Yippee!" Throwing down his rod, he crawled across the grass, threw himself around my waist and gave me the old boa-constrictor squeeze.

You know what? It felt terrific.